A SEAT ON THE SAND

A SEAT ON THE SAND

DAVID FORSYTH

SUNDIAL HOUSE PRESS

A SEAT ON THE SAND

First published in 2018
by SUNDIAL HOUSE PRESS
An imprint of The Sundial Press

The Sundial Press
Sundial House, The Sheeplands, Sherborne, Dorset DT9 4BS

www.sundial-house-press.co.uk

A CIP catalogue record for this book is available from the British Library

ISBN 978-1-908274-77-9

Printed in Great Britain
by 4Edge Limited

CONTENTS

A SEAT ON THE SAND

A holiday casts cares away.
New promises present each day.
Wherever you are your mind feels free
on land or lake, on sand or sea.

Dreamlike was the only way to describe it. The sand on the beach had been baked all day by a sun unusually fierce for England. It was now so hot that the rising heat disturbed the air above it, and everything shimmered … continuously. Even those standing still, or objects such as brollies or deckchairs, seemed to possess their own vague motion when viewed indistinctly through the haze.

I lay back on my deckchair at the top of the beach, placed under a large awning, thoughtfully erected by the deckchair company for that day, and surveyed the crowded scene through half-closed eyelids. Even in the shade the atmosphere was so hot that people flopped in their chairs, too drained of energy to want to move (and so become hotter), and the collective mind became dulled. My level of consciousness seemed to hover somewhere halfway between reality and sleep. Time stood still. I had never felt so relaxed.

Out in the open people sheltered under large umbrellas or lay on towels, smeared with sun cream, and all probably so stuporous that they were unaware of how seriously their skin was suffering. They would know later! Everyone wore sandals or flip-flops because it was unbearable to walk barefoot on the burning sand.

Altogether it was too jolly hot for activity of any sort – except for bathing – and so it was a quiet and peaceful scene, and eventually I drifted into sleep.

Staying in an hotel nearby, and intending to explore the local area, I realised that any such venture on this particular day would be simply too exhausting and unpleasant. So for the first time since my childhood I spent the day on the beach, claiming my spot and occupying a seat on the sand.

When I returned to some degree of wakefulness I found that I was reflecting on a previous sun-drenched holiday that I had taken many years before: 1960, to be exact. Conditions such as these were much more common around the Mediterranean, and in that year I had worked my tent-less way around Italy with friends as a penniless student. We had travelled down the hilly centre of the country, passed through Rome, and were proceeding further south. The heat was always intense and unrelenting, and it was only the numerous, gushing drinking fountains in Rome that had saved us. Being visitors and English we had no siesta, but strolled, saw and suffered.

All this bred in us a longing to be by the sea, but to approach the coast it was either steep cliffs that were unclimbable or a few desirable sandy seafronts owned and enclosed by expensive hotels.

Eventually, we managed to creep down a narrow rocky gap between the high walls of two hotels and reached the beckoning sea six feet below the end of the rock. We dived in, turned round to face the land, and to our horror found ourselves looking up at the opening of a large sewer pipe. No discharge at that moment, but we scrambled out rapidly, wondering whether we had contracted every disease under the sun.

Then our luck was in when we made for Sorrento a little further south along the coast.

At this point the cliffs were hundreds of feet high, sloping steeply down to the sea. To get there we had to abandon the main road and board a local bus. The journey was a hair-raising experience because it had to zigzag downhill around ten or so very acute hairpin bends. As it swung round each corner the passengers fell silent because the front of the bus seemed likely to scrape against the rock the whole of the way round. Tension grew with each successive turn because, although the driver seemed supremely confident, you felt that to maintain such fine judgement was asking too much of him, and that only a very slight miscalculation would bring disaster. But all was well. He had the road to himself, there being no room for any vehicle coming up to pass him. The horn was sounded on and off all the way down to deter anyone from trying.

In the end it was worth the experience. After two hot and sticky weeks journeying inland we had a really refreshing bathe from a rather narrow but stony beach. Lying contentedly in the sun we dried quickly, then rested some more until it was time to find something to eat.

But then came the reckoning.

None of us had been to the Mediterranean before, and did not realise how quickly the sun burnt the skin after a salt-water swim. Being very fair-haired I was affected the most badly. My left leg had been uppermost as I lay there and it now began to swell and I to feel increasingly unwell and feverish.

It was only after the holiday that I learnt that the sea-salt crystals dried onto the skin and then acted as tiny magnifying glasses, concentrating the sun's rays on the skin beneath – as children delight in burning leaves with hand-held magnifying glasses. Nowadays there are often freshwater showers available at resorts to wash the salt off after bathing, to prevent such complications.

So that night we camped on the beach. I was too ill to

move and took two aspirins, passing a wretched night feeling weak and ill.

Next morning I felt just well enough for us to move on to the next place, Salerno, limping slowly because of the swollen leg. There we had an hour to wait before catching a train further south. My friends went to look at an interesting church, but I limped off to find a Gents: a 'Uomini'.

Everywhere else in Italy I had been directed to one close by, but here the population had other ideas. Person after person directed me with a wave of the hand further into the back streets of the town. Eventually I found myself in a narrow passage between two tall buildings barely wide enough to admit one's shoulder's across.

A few yards ahead was one of the fattest women I had ever seen, sitting in a large round metal bath full of water, clearly enjoying a soak. All this seemed very wrong, but I felt too unwell and too desperate to turn away, and paused. Before I could say anything she jerked her thumb over her shoulder and a young woman emerged from a doorway and looked at me enquiringly. I repeated my usual request and she waved to me to follow her into the house.

I entered a long, dim room with beds to right and left, and an aisle between them like a dormitory. Halfway along on the left, in an extra-wide gap between two beds, she opened a low door up to about chest height, revealing a deep recess with a toilet at the rear. She turned away. I could never get inside so I had to reach it from the doorway.

I then thanked her saying "Multo grazie" and tapping my watch urgently I said "El treno" with emphasis to show that time was short.

"Oh no," she said quietly, standing in front of me and gently placing a hand flat on my chest. Clearly she had other ideas with a prospect of a reward afterwards. Feigning not to notice this I thanked her again and repeated the watch gesture and the connection with the train, and limped purposefully out into the sunshine.

The large woman's jaw literally dropped open and she nearly fell out of the bath in her surprise at what she must have thought to be the quickest liaison between man and woman ever known. I nodded to her and limped off to the station with what haste I could muster.

I still felt weak, but fortunately there were only twenty miles by train and bus to Paestum, our furthest point south. There we inspected the group of three Greek temples – the best-preserved in the Mediterranean area and much better than any to be found in Greece – and then made camp in a wood, blissfully cool, that extended down to the beach.

My friends wandered off to the beach that presented a picture never to be forgotten; sky, sea and surrounding low land were a shimmering blend of pastel shades shimmering like the one I was sitting on now: even better – it was totally deserted, this being a rather isolated area.

I rested for a while, then limped after them through the wood along a narrow path. A grey-haired man met me here, noticed my limp, and asked what was wrong. He sounded German. I explained.

"Let me see", he said.

I exposed my left leg.

"Ah yes", he said. "I was a prisoner of the British in Egypt in the war, in Alexandria, and many were affected like this. Go and rest and I will bring some powder to help you."

He was as good as his word. Half-an-hour later he came with a white powder that he applied to the leg, and kept in place by wrapping fine gauze around it like a bandage.

"Always stay in the shade", he advised. "Only leave it in early morning or late evening".

He wished me well, and left.

I never saw him again, but I have often thought of his kindness. Overnight the improvement was quite dramatic. The swelling was much less, the leg more comfortable, I felt better, and after applying more of the powder that he had left me we soon began a train journey taking us far north and to the east, over all that day and the following night.

North Italy had seemed very hot when we had first arrived, but now it seemed a pleasant contrast to the South. There was dew on the grass!

My mind returned to the present day. It was cooler here now, the evening approaching, and the crowd thinning. I must have dozed the afternoon away. I rose stiffly to my feet, stretched, and moved off towards my hotel and its welcome refreshment. A beer, then a good meal with wine. If only we had had this to look forward to after the heat of an Italian day, in the cool of the evening, instead of a cheap bowl of spaghetti and meat sauce. That would really have been the icing on the cake.

IN THE NICK OF TIME

Mike stirred his coffee, then looked across at Jean. "Some of us are to attend a conference next weekend," he said. "It's because our probationary period with thc firm is coming to an end. We will be given talks to bring us up-to-date on anything new, but it's also meant to give us an opportunity to relax away from work, and to chew over anything and everything as the mood takes us. 'Team building' is the phrase. It won't just be us – other building surveyors, at a similar stage of experience, will be there too."

Jean looked up from her cherry tart wryly. She would miss his company. But she nodded, taking it all in good part. She was that kind of girl. After all, once this phase was finished his pay would go up considerably, and they could plan a good-sized flat together and arrange a wedding.

At the time each was in a rather small accommodation, just suitable for one. Jean had completed a secretarial course very creditably, and had succeeded in getting a good job as a P.A. because she had the right attitude. Always calm and presentable she applied herself intelligently, worked hard, and was good at dealing with people – pleasing both them and her boss.

She also had a great sense of humour, and a rather devastating smile could easily appear.

And then along came Mike.

Inevitably they had met at a party. People simply do not get to know each other well while waiting at bus stops or at railway stations. They enjoyed each other's company straight away and meeting again soon seemed to be the most natural thing in the world: inevitable. Nothing else would do.

Jean was slim and attractive with tamed dark hair: the curls always remained in place leaving both hands free all the time. Mike was tall, fair and cheerful good company. Happily they looked forward to marriage and a family, and indulged in pipe dreams such as young couples do. Over many months they felt that each had come to know the other very well, their likes and dislikes, and the way they thought about things. Out of this grew an understanding and respect for each other that boded well for the future. They became engaged.

"We have to drive to the hotel on Friday night," explained Mike. "After the get-together on Saturday there is dinner and an evening of relaxation. Then we return home on Sunday after lunch, when I'll ring you to arrange when we can meet up next."

"I hope that there aren't too many attractive young lady building surveyors," Jean smiled wickedly. "But seriously! I'm sure it will be interesting and a nice change for you. I hope you enjoy it."

The conference duly took place. Once back at home Mike rang Jean, at a later hour than expected.

"Had a good time?" She said.

"Yes. It all went rather well. In the evening some entertainers had been booked to amuse us after dinner for an hour or so, which was fine. After lunch today everyone left, but on the way back I made a detour to look at an attractive and interesting old country house, surrounded by stunning countryside. I'll tell you all about it over lunch."

At the café he explained.

"Two men moved among us, spending some time with each group doing conjuring tricks – the usual things such as card tricks and guessing what you'd write on a piece of paper, etc. A good way of doing it: not too long over each session. They were very good, too! – Oh! By the way, to put the record straight, the conference was entirely male!" he grinned.

"What made you visit this house in the country?"

"It was odd really," said Mike. "I don't really remember why. I suppose someone must have suggested it, but I don't recall who did. Anyway I was convinced enough to make the effort. I seemed to know exactly where to go as well, which surprised me: turning down a country lane halfway through a village, turning right again, and there on the left was this magnificent house set back behind large closed iron gates. An even narrower lane led off round the back, the South side, where I parked and got out. Across a meadow I saw a lawn and flowerbeds surrounding the house. Turning my back on it I beheld the promised view, the land dropping away into fields and woods, and I could see for miles. Really magnificent. I'm glad that I went. Then I came home."

Nearly a week later Mike received a call from his boss to come and see him. In his office stood a man in a grey coat.

"This is Detective-Sergeant Mann who has asked to take the fingerprints of all those from here who attended the conference. This is part of a routine enquiry relating to an incident that took place in the vicinity. It concerns all those who visited the area last weekend."

Mike readily agreed and complied.

On the following Monday his boss summoned him again, this time to meet the sergeant in the vacant seminar room. With him was a detective constable. He was invited to sit.

"Thank you for coming, Sir," said the sergeant. "Following on from our last meeting there are a few questions I must ask you to complete our enquiries. First, could you please give me your name and address."

Mike did so. The constable took notes.

"I understand that you attended the conference last weekend" (details were given). Mile replied in the affirmative.

"Did you go directly from home to the conference, Sir?"

"I did".

"Did you at any time leave the conference, returning later?"

"No".

"I understand that you all departed after lunch on Sunday". Mike nodded.

"Would you mind telling me the make and colour of your car?"

Mike did so. "It's a bright blue – rather too noticeable."

"Now Sir, please tell me what you did between leaving the hotel and arriving home."

The story was repeated just as told to Jean.

"Did you at any point enter the grounds?"

"No. After looking at the view, as impressive as I was promised, I got back in the car and drove home."

"That will be all for now, thank you Sir, but I have been

asked to tell you that the property you looked at was unoccupied at the time. The owners were away on holiday. The caretaker had discovered that a burglary had taken place at the weekend. A silver box, part of the collections stolen, was left behind, and your finger-prints were found on it. I'm going now to the Inspector to report back."

He was looking closely at Mike whose face was frozen into and expression of horrified incredulity.

"I don't understand this at all," he blurted out, "I never went inside or even knew that there was a collection to steal. The strange thing is that I don't even remember who told me about the place and gave me directions."

Once the police had departed Mike went straight to his boss and poured out the horrible story.

"Well Mike, knowing you as I do I find the story incredible. But facts are facts and fingerprints are undeniable evidence. I'll ring the firm's solicitors and we'll go and see them this morning. There's bound to be a summons to attend the magistrate's court very soon."

They were seen by Mr. Perkins of Goodbody, Smart and Messenger, who listened assiduously to their tale.

"Taking your innocence, vehemently professed, as the truth," he remarked slowly, "we have to consider carefully how this might have arisen. There is always the possibility that someone has arranged all this to 'set you up' as the supposed burglar, planting the box where it could easily be found. Do you have anyone so evilly disposed towards you that they would do such a thing?"

"No", said Mike, "I do not have any enemies that I know of."

"The 'fly-in-the-ointment'", continued Mr. Perkins, "is that this was not just any silver box but one that was definitely part of the collection. I had a word with the CID before you came. I think that we will need to take the advice of counsel and have you represented in court. It may come to attendance at the crown court if the magistrates feel unable to decide on the issue."

Which is precisely what happened. Counsel made the case that time was needed to acquire further evidence before a proper defence could be prepared, and a hearing at the crown court was scheduled for a month's time.

Meanwhile Jean and Mike had had a real 'heart-to-heart'. Naturally her faith in Mike had received a jolt over the fingerprint evidence, but his total bewilderment and distress, clearly having no clue about how to even start to prove his innocence, convinced her. She knew in her heart that he would never dream of doing what he was accused of.

So she set her logical mind to the task, calm amid the anguish.

"So, Mike, you knew nothing about this house before the conference. You were only with the others from our firm all evening, and they profess never to have heard of the place. The only strangers you met were the two entertainers, so one of them must have given you the idea of going to see it. Were you ever alone with one or both of them at any stage? Think back to the whole event that evening. Surely anyone being given such detailed information, and remembering it so exactly, must also recall the person and the explanation they gave. How could all that be forgotten?

Mike frowned.

"I remember them leaving one group and then coming over to ours, asking whether we would mind them joining us for a little while. They were very slick, showing us a variety of 'sleight-of-hand' tricks such as making things in their hands disappear and reappear. Of course, we had had a good bit to drink before and during the meal, and so were willing customers and no doubt more easily deceived. They were very good at handling cards. Oh yes! Now I vaguely remember! At one point, to show that there was no cheating, I was handed a metal box with cards inside it and asked to take them out and shuffle them. Well – I suppose it could have been silver."

"After that my memory is rather vague. One of them took me to a table to show me a last turn because the others where deep in discussion about card-sharping. It was the old, old trick of three inverted large eggcups placed in a line. A dice was placed under one. Then they were moved about quite quickly so that their places in the line changed. The puzzle was to choose which eggcup hid the dice. I never seemed to get it right, and had to try and concentrate harder and harder. I don't remember whether I ever succeeded."

Jean thought for a minute or so. Some ideas had come to her. A time for discussion was over. She must now play a lone hand, following her hunches as unobtrusively as possible. Only when she had dug up some new facts and laid the ground would the forces of law be called upon to help.

First she rang the hotel, praising the evening's entertainment, and discovered the address and phone number of the agency that supplied them. Next she arranged to call at the agency expressing interest in the two men for future purposes and the range of their expertise.

"Ah, the hypnotists!" they said, pointing out that this particular skill had not been required to be demonstrated on this occasion. They detailed what else they could do. She asked whether they were hired widely and was given a list of recent venues mostly at weekends. "Naturally," she said, "I was not present at the conference, but I would like to see them in action myself." Where were they appearing next?

Armed with all this information Jean departed for a rapid think. It had been a stroke of luck to learn that they were hypnotists, and this fitted in with what she felt was happening during Mike's description of the eggcup episode, of him being progressively mesmerised to the point where he lost awareness. That would be the time when information would be fed into his subconscious. He must have been identified as a suitable subject for hypnosis and so was the one to be handed the metal box first.

This would mean that the entertainers had already burgled the house to obtain the box, and subsequently returned it. This, and Mike's presence near the house, would make him the prime suspect. Mr. Perkins had discovered from the CID that a local farmer inspecting his livestock in a nearby field had spotted Mike's car parked in the narrow lane – and that it went away after five to ten minutes.

For some reason the police had not investigated the entertainers as the possible culprits. The problem was to prove that they were. It would be too obvious if they were to pass on the collection at once, being an easily recognised whole. It would have to be disposed of piecemeal over a period of time. The hope must be that it would be retained by them at their houses, or somewhere owned by them. If any formal approach were made to search these premises the loot would disappear rapidly before this took place. It would have to be a sudden raid on some pretext or other – a supposed tip-off about drugs or money laundering – and preferably when they were away. Her knowledge of the next venue would make it the ideal time.

She talked this over with Mike who was overwhelmed by her belief in him, and by her ingenuity and effort on his behalf. They gained an appointment with the solicitor, and he in turn discussed the matter with counsel. They agreed that this was the only possible way that they could see to escape from the dilemma and try to solve the case.

Would the police cooperate?

The inspector received the deputation of Mr. Perkins and of counsel and then went to see the superintendent. He went in turn to the chief constable, and they decided to act on the day of the next venue.

Ever since Mike had been placed under suspicion he and Jean had been too disturbed to work properly, and both had been granted some holiday leave. In one sense it was even worse having nothing to do, nothing to occupy their minds, and both had lost weight.

Now there was only half a week to wait. The tension mounted. Neither could sleep the night before the raid. During the next morning they sat by Mike's phone.

Late afternoon. The phone buzzed. Mike lifted the receiver. It was Mr. Perkins. "Good news!" he said. "Some of the collection has been found in one of the houses so you would appear to be in the clear. Quite a lot of other valuables had been found, and the police are now urgently looking at burglaries that took place in the vicinity of their previous venues that you listed. So well done! We now await the charging of the entertainers and to see whether they will confess or insist on a trial. If the latter case, you will be called as a witness."

But all was well. They confessed. In shear relief at the release from tension first Jean, then Mike, shook, and the tears flowed to release their pent-up emotion.

The Inspector came round and thanked Jean for her clever assistance and suggested, with a grin, that she might like to join the CID. "In the nick of time," he quipped, "you saved him from being put in the 'nick'!"

Mike's colleagues threw a party for them to celebrate the happy outcome. As they entered the room as guests there was a loud burst of clapping, and the DJ thundered out that rousing, catchy song: 'Stand by your man'!

Parties are parties, but this one had a real purpose to it and it went well. Mike announced that they were bringing forward the date of the wedding, and all were to be invited.

But next week ... back to work!

THE CARTOONIST

I was born in a small town high upon the central hills in Italy very – oh, so very – far above the plains below. From its massive western gateway, or when walking close to the high walls either side of it, the views to the far distance were magnificent. Large olive groves and corn fields studded the slopes down to the valley, and along its bottom could be seen a river, a railway and many ribbons of road. Beyond that a mistiness veiled the lower hills on the far side.

Apart from people walking the dusty roads, and the squeaking axles of the ox-carts in the fields and farmyards, the scene was one huge panorama of peace.

This was the course of my young life. Nothing much seemed to happen, and everyday saw the same routines. We rose soon after dawn for breakfast. The women aired bedding on the verandas, washed clothing and hung it out to dry, then shopped for food. Men went about their work early, and as a child I attended school.

In the afternoon it was too hot to do anything and everyone retired indoors, the windows shuttered to keep out the sun. As the air cooled outside people emerged for a more active and sociable evening.

Then it was that I would meet my friends. We ran and played along the cobbled streets, or ventured outside the walls and explored the mysteries of those wooded areas nearby. I enjoyed this time of day most, not just because the air was pleasant but because, above all, I relished talking with my companions, ruminating on anything that came to our collective mind. School never held much appeal, with only its set subjects being rigorously pursued. So I never applied myself ardently, or excelled at anything – except art.

I drew well and was praised for it. Discussion and doodling were my favourite pastimes.

My friends were always amused by my caricatures of people whom we knew well – the mayor, town characters of note, the school masters, and of the friends themselves – especially when showing them striking poses that were typical of them – or just imagined.

Allowing my mind to roam freely, following through the themes of our conversations, or creating my pictures, was when I felt most happy. Far preferable to the lessons in school that seemed to me to be such a constraint.

My parents were elderly and had no other children. They managed a bakery and a small general store in which I helped as I grew older. When I was in my late teens they retired, and I went to work in a small bookshop that also sold stationary and catered for the tourists' appetite for information, local and general.

My circle of friends gradually diminished as many now had their own jobs and pursuits, or had moved to nearby towns or villages, but I still whiled away some of the evenings in cafés mulling over the problems of the world with those who savoured trying to reason and find solutions. I envied the men who had retired and then seemed to spend hours at tables around the town's square, sipping coffee or something stronger, and passing comment on everyone and everything that came to mind.

So on those evenings when I was on my own I would stroll out through the main gate and pace along by the walls, as others did, taking in the view. At intervals there were benches where people could sit and contemplate rather than indulge in perpetual motion.

When a bench was empty I would sit and sketch – I always brought my paper, pens and pencils in a shoulder bag. My favourite bench was sometimes occupied by an elderly man with a walking stick. When this happened I would walk by.

One day I was sitting there and soon became absorbed in my drawing. Suddenly I was startled by a voice over my shoulder: "if you don't my saying so," it said, "you have talent!"

I turned and beheld the elderly gentleman who often

sat there. I rose, but he waved to me to be seated and asked whether I would mind if he sat down for a short while. Of course, I agreed.

"May I look more closely at what you have drawn?" he asked.

I handed over my pad. The picture was entirely imaginary. A man was bent over some flowers in a public park. He held some blooms that he had picked, but was looking up in guilt at a man standing before him who was looking most disapproving, and wagging an admonitory finger.

After a minute he returned the pad, "very neat, and the meaning is immediately clear", he praised. "Elegantly executed. Do you draw for a living?"

"Oh no! I draw for fun", I replied. Then I explained the nature of my job.

He was silent for a few minutes. We both sat still and gazed at the view, lost in our own thoughts.

Eventually he stirred.

"I'll tell you what I do," he offered. "It is some years since I worked for a living, and I'm comfortably off. I'm alone now since my wife died some years ago and there were no children. So to keep in touch with the world I communicate with it by writing articles on any matter that I happen to be pondering upon at the time. These are printed regularly in a periodical in the next town to the north. It comes out every fortnight".

"In fact," he continued thoughtfully, "it is more a conversation because people respond to it in the next issue. The rest of the paper concerns local issues and advertisements. I have been doing this for some years."

"Looking at your work has brought to mind how much more interesting and appealing my contribution would be if accompanied by a picture, or cartoon, to highlight the main thrust of the article. You could provide this. If you read my finished work before it went to press, then matched it with your drawing, they could be sent off together. With your permission I'll speak to the editor. I feel sure he would agree since it would enhance his presentation. Of course, you would be paid."

There was silence for a minute or two as I was allowed to think about it. This did not take long. The two things that gave me pleasure, sketching and mulling over any subject under the sun, would both be involved.

I turned to him.

"This sounds to be a very exciting idea," I said slowly. "It appeals to me very much". Then I tolkd him about my lifelong love of discussion."

"In fact", I confessed, "I would never have thought of seeking out such a possibility myself. I can hardly believe that this offer has come 'out of the blue'. If the editor agrees I would like to give it a go."

"Very well," he said. "Let's try it. I live here." He handed me his card with his name and address. "The latest issue has just gone out, so why not meet me here in a week and I will hand over my next article. You can make your sketch at leisure, and then come to my house and we can discuss it."

The next week went by – very slowly, it seemed. For me life suddenly had a sense of purpose. I was excited, but at the same time anxious in case the whole project fell through. The editor might not agree. My drawing may not match up to what is required.

The day came. In the evening I arrived at the bench at the appointed time to find him already there. I expect that I looked strained because he smiled and calmed my fears at once. "It's fine," he said, "the editor is very keen."

I took a big breath and relaxed.

From a leather folder he took some typed sheets and handed them to me:

"Read them while we sit here. When you're ready we could discuss what you're drawing might highlight."

I sat back in the warm evening and applied myself in earnest, hoping that ideas would occur.

The article was a dissertation on food prices and food waste. Nothing much could be done about the prices, but something could about the ingrained idea that everything eaten, cooked or not, should be bought fresh that day. This meant that if not all of these fresh fruit and vegetables were needed to be prepared for the table, the excess was thrown away. Over a week this waste amounted to a great deal. Since everything was bought by the kilo this represented money thrown away.

He then launched into the idea of buying enough for meals for two or three days, using everything up, and preserving dishes in the fridge or freezer until required.

Of particular concern was bread, which formed a large part of the daily diet, but of which a considerable amount was discarded. It had to be fresh, being of a type that would be too dry if kept until the next day. But the price reflected the size of the loaf so this was another example of the steady drain of money to the rubbish bins. He advocated a simple answer – that in general the loaves should be smaller, but concluded that it was up to the bakers to 'play ball' to help their customers.

I thought for a moment, then took out my sketch pad and pencil, and made a rough drawing as follows. A woman had sliced a large loaf on the kitchen table. A few slices that she did not need were being pushed to one end where they were toppling over to fall into a waste bin on the floor. As they were starting to fall they tuned into coins, and it was these that were going into the bin. Money was being thrown away.

I handed this to the old man.

He studied it for a minute.

"This is perfect," he exclaimed. He turned to me with a keen glance. "It goes straight to the heart of the matter. The message is crystal-clear to anyone. Well done indeed, and so quickly! Take it home, make a fair copy, bring it to me tomorrow and all will go straight off by post."

So with warm smiles of satisfaction we returned to the gate and went our separate ways.

Sure enough they were printed in the next issue.

I obtained my copy because my shop sold the periodical. The old man showed me the editor's letter and the amount offered me, to which I readily agreed. The cheque covered both of us and I was given my share. I was exhilarated. I had joined the rest of the world and felt very much a part of it.

The next few months went smoothly by, the cartoons complementing the articles successfully. But sometimes the old man did not turn up at the bench. Going to his house I discovered that he had become less steady on his feet and was now no longer confident that he could make the journey. From then on I went to his house as a matter of course.

One day, nearly a year after I had begun the venture, I found him sitting at home looking distressed and rather sad.

"I just don't seem able to concentrate properly any more," he sighed. "I've tried several times but no suitable subject springs to mind and my writing simply dries up. I'm very sorry, but I'm going to have to give it all up. So you will have to do so as well."

I felt distraught – for both of us.

Then, with a surge of hope, and my mind suddenly keyed up, I saw my chance.

"Will you let me write this week's article?" I offered. "Don't tell the editor yet, but see if it is accepted. I'll add the usual cartoon. If this works, and you still find that you'd rather not do any more, then I might be able to carry on the tradition that you started. Our combined efforts increase the circulation and I might succeed in maintaining this new popularity. At least it's worth giving it a try."

He nodded tiredly, then smiled. "Why not? Have a go and we'll see what happens."

Three issues followed without comment from the other end. Finally the old man decided to write to the editor and 'spill the beans'. The upshot was that I was asked to go and see him, and met him in the office in his house. He was most cordial, and clearly as old as my friend. He expressed his delight that the paper could carry on as before, and after the last three issues he felt assured it would.

Before I left he explained how he built up each edition, showing me the detail of all his contacts for advertisements and local news, and how it all worked.

"As with your friend," he explained, "I have no family, and this has been my life's work. When I retire in a year or so I would be devastated if all that I had built up were to come to a sudden end, and all the readers left with nothing."

He looked at me steadily, blinking and sitting very still, as though trying to make up his mind. Then taking a big breath he spoke slowly and very seriously.

"Far be it from me to influence the course of your life," he said, "but you seem to fit into the paper world so well. It seems to be just the thing for you. I have no obvious successor, and a new and unknown editor may alter things in a way that neither I nor my readers would want: I expect that it might become very different from what it is now."

"If you were to work with me over the next year, learning the trade, I would then be happy to turn the whole project over to you, as your own, to develop as you wish. I have sufficient for my wants and would not need any payment or pension. Then I could sit back with a settled and contented mind, and watch from the sidelines."

"Please think about it. Maybe you will want some time to decide whether you want to do this or not."

I simply stared at him. This would be an opportunity beyond my wildest dreams, and a gift at that. I felt stunned, but a surge of excitement welled up.

"Quite frankly," I said (my voice was rather strained) "there is nothing that I would like more. I'm overwhelmed and can hardly believe it. I know that I want to accept your offer without any hesitation. I'm very, very grateful, and don't know how to thank you enough – except that I'll fulfil your wishes."

I sat still and tense, my heart thudding, but then he visibly relaxed and smiled.

"I expect you are feeling rather shocked by all this," he said. "But I'm delighted, and all my anxieties are laid low. It being a full-time job means that you will have to give up the job in the bookshop."

I went home with my head in a spin. On the way I sat on the bench and stared into space. It was here that the emotion, churning under the surface, got the better of me at last, and the tears flowed.

I threw myself into this new venture with gusto. More and more I was left to manage things myself. Through contact with my old friends I was provided with local news from the towns and villages to which they had moved, and so increased the sales more widely. I also prevailed upon experts in various fields to provide useful and interesting articles about their trades, with something to appeal to everyone: DIY, cooking, plumbing, fishing and gardening, to name a few, and also creative advice on such as dress-making, knitting, curtain fitting and the use of sewing machines. The shops were pleased because they could sell all the material and equipment now sought after.

Finally came the icing on the cake. I applied for a secretary and one of my friends asked if his sister might be considered. When she arrived I simply knew at once that she was the girl for me. If not love at first sight, then it certainly was so five minutes later!

We are married now, with three children. The business goes well. When my old friend died he made me his heir, looking upon me as the son he never had. I had a plaque affixed to the bench in his memory.

Often we sit there on a fine evening and reflect on our good fortune: that you never know what is just around the corner, and on the importance of having the courage to seize opportunities when they arise. Of these I seem to have had more than my fair share.

THE AMBROSE HOTEL

I should never have come. I knew that now. Not in weather like this. The forecast had been rain, gusting gale-force winds, and worsening: but not as ferocious as this. Sheets of water sluiced down the windscreen, obscuring the view, and the wipers were of little help. Visibility was limited to brief glimpses only, courtesy of the squalls that buffeted the curtain of water and the car.

These moments revealed the narrow, twisting country road, rising and falling, and the high banks on either side crowded with a dense mass of tall trees, the wildly whipping branches threatening to part company from the trunks. Although only 4.30 in the afternoon, outside it was as black as night, making driving a nightmare. But it would be dangerous to stop and there were no side-turnings.

Knowing that I was nearly there I kept glancing keenly to the right to catch sight of the two lamps, one on the top of each pillar, that would indicate the gateway to The Ambrose Hotel. In this murk they would be hard to see. But suddenly they were there, dimly seen, and with relief I turned cautiously between them.

Immediately the scene reminded me of the start of a TV mystery thriller: a misty view of the tall wrought-iron gates on either side, large bushes jerked to 'and fro' by the wind, and behind these swayed tall trees through which I could hear the wind howling and moaning. At that moment a flash of lightening lit the scene like a frozen sepia 'still' of yesteryear.

Ahead loomed a large building. As I entered a gravelled forecourt, I joined a line of cars parked facing it. My lights had picked out the unusually dark green of the car next to me, and looking up I saw its owner hastening up broad stone steps to a covered porch, suitcase in hand. He rang a bell, was swiftly admitted, and the door closed behind him.

I stared with interest at the broad, heavy-looking stone building, three stories high. To the left there were some lower extensions and maybe outbuildings vaguely visible through the gloom. To the right there was one long, windowless addition, about two stories high. A narrow lawn disappeared around this, fringed by the continuous belt of wind-swept trees.

There was no point in any further delay. I would have to make a dash for it. Luckily I wore a long coat and had an old trilby to cram down on my head. The door had to be forced open against the wind, and once outside it was difficult to stand. I grabbed my case from the back seat, locked the car, and headed unsteadily for the door.

Once inside the contrast could not have been greater. Immediately bathed in warmth and pleasant low lighting tension and discomfort drained away, the heavy door and thick walls muffling the rage of the tempest outside. The porter took my case over to the reception desk on the right and placed it on the floor.

I glanced around the large hall that rose the full two stories above. To the left were two open doors, and beyond these a passage leading to the back of the house and distant kitchen noises of clatter and chatter. Directly across stood a large grandfather clock. To the right of this was the grand staircase, two steps up and then a right turn onto a flight that led up to the landing that ran right round the next three sides. From there another flight led up to a similar arrangement on the second floor. Halfway along each side-landing a corridor branched off, presumably to the rooms.

I completed the formalities and was taken to my room on the first floor overlooking the drive. No more cars had arrived, but the view was still horrific and I drew the brocade curtains. The room and 'en-suite' were spacious, well-appointed and warm. I was impressed. Sitting on the bed I reached for the 'phone and rang my wife who would be anxious to know that I had arrived safely. She had gone away for a few days to look after her sister who had had a recent operation, and had suggested that I also take a break from home and the work at my surgery. As luck would have it a partner could swap weekend duties with me. He wanted a free one later in order to fulfil some hoped-for engagement.

I had chosen this hotel because of the following recommendation by a friend: "Comfort, good food, friendly staff and a feeling of being completely cut off from the rest of the world" were his reasons. It had sounded good. There were hills all round to be walked and the coast only another valley away.

"Carole?"

"Hello David! So you've arrived. I heard about the storm. It must have been a terrible journey!"

"It was", I replied, "especially the last hour or so, but thankfully that's all over now. I'm very pleased with the hotel – warm, welcoming and comfortable. Dinner in an hour and half or so. How's Jane?"

"Making progress. Should be getting about soon"

"Good news! I'll phone tomorrow after a good rest. Bye for now."

A good rest! How lucky that I could not see into the future!

The bar was entered through the first of the hall doors. The windows faced the drive, the curtains were drawn and the tables well spaced out. Four couples were present in the room and a man sat reading at a table against the opposite wall. I collected a drink from a pleasant barman standing behind the bar on the right, a newspaper from a rack, and settled at a small table near the door.

Ten minutes later a tall man came in and I recognised the owner of the green car. He looked round and smiled at me and nodded.

"I arrived just after you," I said. "Did you have a terrible journey too?"

"Not one that I wish to remember!" He nodded again, collected a drink and a paper and chose his table.

After a while a waiter appeared through some double doors by the bar and announced that the dining room was ready if we would care to come through at our leisure. The four couples rose and we three men joined the procession. In the room were twelve elegantly dressed tables. Double doors on the left opened into the kitchen area, and one on the right was ajar and led into the passage, where a board indicated that the cloakrooms were nearby.

The meal was excellent, as was the service, and the courses came and went. The windows looked to the rear but the curtains were closed. After an interval the Head Waiter announced that coffee and after-dinner drinks would be served in the lounge when we were ready, and in two or three minutes we were following him into the passage, left past the cloakrooms, and then a right turn into a covered way across the back of the house.

Here the windows were uncovered, and after the

warmth and good food the sight, across a narrow strip of lawn, of trees still in the grip of the storm, rather dispelled the recent feeling of relaxation and contentment.

The waiter pulled open a door at the end of the passage and we filed through – then all stood as one to stare in surprise at the room. It was huge and high – about two stories or so – and the walls were windowless. Two dormer windows in the pitched roof would be the only source of light by day. Armchairs and sofas surrounded low tables. At the far end was a well-stocked bar, and a waitress stood by a trolley with everything on it needed to serve coffee. At our end a cavernous stone fireplace contained an electric stove giving the impression of a log fire.

The waiter explained that this room had been a barn that had been joined to the house over four hundred years ago to become the grand dining hall. He warned us that the door on the other side of the fireplace was false – bricked up behind. It had been the original entrance, but did not suit the layout of the hotel when it was designed earlier in the present century.

The couples selected tables. It seemed natural for we three men to sit together, which we did by the fire. Coffee was served and the waiter served drinks.

We introduced ourselves.

"I'm David Gardner," I said, and told my story. The green car man was John Robertson, a solicitor, on his way to stay for a few days with an old friend who had recently lost his wife. The third man was Simon Arbuthnot, a publisher, on his way to a book fair. Both were there for one night only and had come on recommendation, as I had, and we were all delighted that the hotel lived up to its reputation.

One by one the couples drifted off to their rooms, and we were left alone. The waiter announced that he was going off duty but we would be welcome to help ourselves to any further drinks and make a note of them and our room numbers on the pad on the bar. If needed there was a night manager resident on the other side of the hotel.

As he left the room the din of the storm came clearly through the open door. None of us felt like retiring yet, so we fetched another drink and sat in a reminiscent mood discussing extremes of weather we had known and past discomforts experienced.

And then it happened.

A sudden and almighty crash.

We froze, looking at each other, then round the room. No sign of anything wrong. The lights were steady.

Sensing that it had been on the side we came in I rose and went to the door. Remembering that it opened outwards I turned the handle and pushed. There was no movement. I put my shoulder to it and it moved only a few inches, but enough to see through the gap the rough bark of a large tree branch: one that only a chain saw would shift. The storm had clearly uprooted a tree and we were trapped. No phone. No cloakroom. No other means of exit. I turned to the others and explained.

I will always remember John rising to his feet the next moment and facing us with his back to the fireplace.

"It seems as though we may be trapped here for the night", he said. "But there could be one possible solution, though I don't know whether it still exists. This place was taken over in the war as a training centre for agents, and that was when I was last here. A Roman Catholic family had lived here for generations, and when the fireplace and chimney were built the opportunity was taken to create a priest hole – more than that, it was also a route of escape. I was shown it once. I'll see if it's still there"

He turned to face the side of the fireplace nearer the trapped door. It was a single, broad slab of stone topped by a row of decorative stone knobs. He tried to work one loose without success. Then he removed a shoe and tapped the knob on all sides with the heel. This time it could be drawn upwards to reveal a stone peg.

"This locks the stone", he explained.

Then seizing the slab by the inner edge he pulled it outwards like a door, hinged top and bottom by stony protrusions slotted into the stone above and below. A dark cavity appeared.

He replaced his shoe and put his head into the gap.

"The air is fresh," he said. "There is a through draught from outside to a gap in the chimney higher up."

I handed him the pencil torch that I always carry as part of my professional equipment – you never know when it comes in useful!

His explanation continued.

"There is a narrow staircase leading down to a small room, both brick-lined. At the far end of the room it passes under the wall. Standing on a brick step that is there, a paving slab above can be pushed up and over like a trap door. There is a path of slabs surrounding this room so it doesn't look out of place."

He entered the doorway and declared that the room was empty, and shone the torch on the steps and we followed him down. Now the storm could be heard in all its fury. John mounted the far step and heaved the slab up and over, immediately being soaked by the rain. Pressing down on the slabs on either side he heaved himself up and scrambled onto the grass. Quickly helping us up, he replaced the slab.

The rain and wind hit us very hard. We were soaked in no time. With as much haste as we could, without slipping, we followed the path round to the front porch.

A prolonged ring brought the night manager in two or three minutes. There must have been an extension to his room.

For a second or two he stared in amazement at the three bedraggled figures, then ushered us quickly inside. We explained. Then all went in a body to the covered way and beheld the tree. The manager closed the door from there to the passage to shut out the rain and wind, and we retreated to the hall and warmth.

He was full of regrets and apologies and was there anything he could do? We elected for a bath and bed, and he said he would ring the General Manager immediately though clearly nothing could be done until the morning.

Morning brought a clear blue sky and sunshine. The storm had abated, and we enjoyed a good breakfast sitting together at the same table.

The waiter invited us to see the manager in his room by the reception desk at our convenience. The call was made from there and we were invited in and seated.

He offered more apologies and the hope that we had managed some sleep. He had not known about the priest hole. He insisted that we would not be presented with bills for our night's stay, and could he perhaps meet the cost of cleaning our suits? Firms would be attending that day to remove the tree and repair the passage.

We thanked him for his offer but said that we would attend to the suits ourselves; then took the opportunity to praise the hotel in all respects.

I declined to stay the second night, deciding to seek out a pleasant hostelry on the coast, well clear of any trees. Promising to keep in touch we went our separate ways, later to bring news of the drama to our families. The wires would be buzzing that night!

Life hangs by a thread . . .

The stories of a 'near-death experience' are as many and as varied as those that end in death. But in the former there is an element of drama because of the narrow line between survival and a fatal outcome. That difference may be due to chance, to a 'sixth sense', to a rapid avoiding-action or to being given the right care in the right place at the right time.

There is the split-second escape. Extending far out from the vehicle's side a lorry's wing mirror narrowly misses the heads of those walking on the pavement, innocently unaware of how near they came to disaster. Equally fortunate are those nearly run down by a car that mounts the kerb.

Sometimes it may be chance that prevents death, but at a distance. To their great annoyance someone fails to arrive at the airport in time to catch their flight, but later hears in horror that the 'plane crashed with no survivors.

All too familiar are those agonising cases that are not immediately fatal, but which are followed by a long drawn-out period during which survival hangs in the balance before final salvation. Such are injures that arise from accidents – a car crash, a fall down a cliff, a terrorist action – or falling prey to a prolonged and potentially fatal illness.

A KITE CATASTROPHE

20,000 volts – but I still lived – thanks to dramatic action that saved my life, and gave me a chance to recover. But what followed was a road leading only to inevitable disaster, a long and bumpy road, and it took drastic action again at the eleventh hour to save the day.

I was eleven years old. My father had given me a present of an old RAF Box Kite, the type that was flown from a rubber dinghy to attract rescuers after an aircraft had ditched in the sea. The metal rods that would form the frame, and the fine yellow canvas that would clothe it, were packed in a yellow sleeve-like bag. There was a separate reel, also yellow. This consisted of a round, yellow metal plate, on one side of which was attached a thick leather handle by which it could be held. On the other side was a revolving drum that could be turned by a handle shaped like a dog-leg. Around it was wound a metal cable.

Once assembled the kite became a hollow box, square at the ends and longer at the sides. The bright yellow canvas was fastened all round each side but not over the ends. Halfway along one of the side-rods there was an attachment for the cable. As it was unwound the sea breeze would carry the kite aloft.

Our garden was most unsuitable for flying a kite: not much breeze compared with the sea, and too many trees, bushes, flowerbeds and vegetable plots – beautiful though they were. I needed an open space over which to run to get it airborne.

One sunny Sunday morning I had enjoyed putting it all together when it suddenly came to me that the huge field next to our garden, then lying fallow and sloping gently up to a coppice, was an ideal place to fly it. My mother was busy in the house and minding my little sister, not yet two, and my father, an eye surgeon, was at the hospital reviewing the cases that he had operated on; so accompanied by my four year old brother I went into the field.

There I unwound about half the cable, then holding the reel in my left hand and gripping the cable in my right I ran forward towards the coppice. The last thing I remember was the thrill of seeing the kite rise up and fly as I had always hoped it would.

When I was next aware of anything it was of something vague and disjointed. My thought processes were non-existent except that I felt that I was on my back surrounded by blackness. There were only scattered flashes of vision of a kaleidoscopic nature. I could hear better than see, and what I heard was my father's voice close above me: I slowly became aware that he was kneeling and bending over me. Soon I had a vague impression of his face.

He was saying: "It's alright, David. You'll be alright. You've had an accident with the kite, but don't worry, we'll soon have you home. Mummy has gone to get a rug and we'll carry you."

After that I was barely conscious but then sensed that I was being carried, suspended in a rug, a person at each end holding the corners.

When next I 'came to' I was lying on the settee in the sitting room, the rug wrapped round me, and the most terrible intense and stinging pain in my chest, right hand and right foot: really unbearable. I saw my mother beside me and managed to tell her about the pain. She said that the doctor would be here very soon and deal with it.

Looking back on it all now I don't know how she managed to look so calm and smile so confidently and reassuringly: it made me feel that all would be well. But, alas, this was not to be so – by a long chalk!

The doctor suddenly seemed to be there, a large and kindly man, with intelligent eyes and a prominent bushy moustache. His manner exuded calm and competence. He had a quiet and soothing voice. He listened to my chest without moving the rug then gave me an injection of morphia to kill the pain. What a relief as the pain began to go, and I felt sleepily relaxed!

I must have slept after that because the next I knew I

was riding in an ambulance on a stretcher with my mother sitting on the other side. We were on our way to the Children's Hospital in Birmingham. How she got back I don't know but possibly my father fetched her, having enlisted the help of the gardener and his wife to look after my brother and sister at the house until they returned.

Later I was given the following detail of what happened up to that point.

A row of telegraph poles ran up the centre of the field and entered the coppice, carrying cables. At a casual glance they would appear to be telephone lines, but in fact were electric cables. Just beyond the coppice was the former home of Stanley Baldwin, when prime minister before the war. The electric power supply to his house had failed and an emergency cable was hastily run up to it across this field. Unfortunately it was uninsulated, and when my kite cable touched it a current of 20,000 volts was earthed through me. Fortunately the cable was burnt through instantaneously and the rest of the cable fell to the ground. Had this not happened I would not be writing this now. The kite flew off and was eventually found over a mile away.

The physical results of this electrocution were horrifying. The sudden muscle contraction it induced brought the reel hard against my chest, over my heart, burning the flesh in depth over a six-inch-plus area. The cable in my right hand had been gripped so tightly that deep trenches were burned in the palm. The skin down all of my right side and leg was brown, and a hole was burned in the skin below the ball of my right foot, and in the sole of the sandal below it, where the current had earthed.

Seeing me lying smoking on the ground my brother ran screaming through the hedge and my father, who fortunately had just returned from the hospital, rushed out because it sounded so urgent. My brother pointed at me.

He found that my heart had stopped and managed to get it going again, so between them they had saved my life. He then called to my mother to bring a rug.

Once I was in the house my father rang the doctor and he came at once, and was seen leaving Stourport-on-Severn, where he lived three-and-a-half miles away crossing the bridge at sixty miles an hour.

He had to be very insistent but I went to the Children's Hospital, clearly the most appropriate place, rather than on an adult ward in another hospital which was being suggested.

Then followed the most agonising three or four weeks of my life. The nurses could not have been kinder but the dressings had to be changed daily over all the areas mentioned above, and because they always stuck hard to me they had to be peeled off, each move a searing pain. I'm sure they felt badly about having to do this, and it must have been a heart-rending task for them, but it simply had to be done to try to prevent infection. After a week or two of this they sat me in a well-filled bath and removed the dressings under water because it was thought to be easier for me. But it didn't make much difference.

I was also given injections morning and evening – probably penicillin and sulphonamides because there was not much else in those days, and my rear became a very painful pin cushion – worse than today because then they used thick, stainless steel needles that had to be sterilized, sharpened and re-used. These had not yet been replaced by the slim disposable ones of today.

In the end the inevitable happened. Most of the wounded flesh was so damaged that it had no blood supply and gangrene set in. I began to feel very tired and ill. Only the removal of all this diseased tissue could save me. If life may hang by a thread, as the saying goes, then this one was becoming a very thin one indeed.

One day a short, spare man in a very neat brown suit, whose hair and small neat moustache were gingery, came to see me and sat casually on the windowsill by my bed. He said that he would be operating on me next day to put everything right and stop the need for anymore dressings. Then he went away.

I learnt later that he was Professor Mansfield, a very skilled plastic surgeon. By that time I was feeling very unwell and was helped to stand at the window by the nurses to wave to my mother, brother and sister on the lawn below. They could not come to the ward because of the infection. This operation was in no way guaranteed to succeed, but very much a 'last chance' event, and years later my mother admitted that that view of me might have been the last time that they would ever see me.

But the prospect that this operation might solve everything, and the dreadful dressings and injections be dispensed with, gave me a surge of hope and I was eager for the next day to come.

As my eyes slowly opened after the operation I felt very relaxed and comfortable, something that I had not felt for a long time, and somehow knew that I was on the road to recovery. I felt very sleepy. Soon I made out a hazy figure standing by the bed, and knew that it was my father in an overcoat.

He said: "Hello David. It's all over now and all is well."

I murmured: "Hello Daddy."

I felt so happy. Then he left.

Over the next few days there was rapid progress. Loose gauze sheets, pads or bandages, all powdered, covered the operation sites. The skin around the left side of my chest had been freed and drawn together, forming a scar that was a question mark in reverse.

I was unable to walk until the skin graft over the ball of my right big toe had healed, so I was taken to the hospital sunday school (only once) in a wheelchair, where I sang

"All Things Bright and Beautiful" rather self-consciously with much younger children.

Soon I was home. It was winter. I had missed the winter term at school. I also had to miss the spring term and stay at home until my health had fully recovered, and when those areas that had had plastic surgery were considered able to withstand the rigours of school life.

When I started school again in the summer I found that the electrocution had wiped away any memory of the detail that I had learned in such subjects as maths, latin and french. The school had been forewarned about this, as I had, and I received much one-to-one teaching at first.

But the interesting and pleasing discovery was that I could now learn more quickly, and concentrate and retain knowledge much more readily than was the case before the accident. All my old misconceptions in these subjects had disappeared, and with this fresh approach I seemed to acquire a much better grasp of everything than before.

Whether this was due to the electrocution or simply the fresh start after a long gap will never be known, but since then I have never looked back.

The nice ending to the story is that my brother was rewarded for saving my life. He had long yearned for a bus conductor's outfit – complete with hat and a ticket-clipping machine. My parents bought it and I thanked him and presented it to him. He was thrilled and didn't stop smiling for days.

COAST AND CURRENTS

Sea sailing sounds idyllic. A stiff breeze, the sails set, the sun shining, and the effortless slicing through the waves as the water hisses along the hull. And so it often is. But not always. It can be rough, sunless, cold and a very wet experience, with exhausting work hauling on the sheets to readjust the sails – difficult when the waves are large and each jars the boat as it bounces up and down.

One must be prepared for all this. Nevertheless it can be enjoyable, especially being confident that the skipper and crew know the boat and the area well: the coast, the hidden rocks below the surface, the competing forces of the tides and currents, and the times of day or night that they occur. Preparation is everything!

As a teenager I was lucky because my family rented a house for a month in the summer at Trearddur Bay in Anglesey. There was a good-sized sailing club, with fourteen-foot clinker-built boats especially designed for the club and made in Bangor. They all had red sails and looked smart.

Our house was on a large headland that lay between

the wide sandy bay to the north and the small bay to the south. This last was where the boats were moored. It had a small and rather gritty beach and was framed by low cliffs that extended in parallel from each end of it straight out to the open sea. In the centre of the entrance was a large rocky island, creating a north and a south passage on either side of it, through one of which the boats could sail according to the tides and winds.

Being on the west coast Anglesey always had interesting weather and seas. Very hot, perfect days for being on the beach were few. The prevailing west wind made it cooler, and because of the wind a wind-break was often necessary if one were not moving about. So it was often a blowy day, the waves large and white-capped, and these made bathing, and certainly sailing, more exciting and a challenge.

The boats sailed round to the large bay for the races in the summer season when the weather permitted. There, on the headland, was a large flagpole rising out of a stone platform that was surrounded by a low stone wall. From it a small cannon faced north across the bay. On the far side of the bay were copious low rocks. To one of them, nearest to the deep water that lay between them and the flagpole, a large metal pole and its supports were bolted. The invisible line between the two poles was both the start line and where the boats finished. The course was marked out by buoys anchored far out in the bay.

The starts were always intriguing to watch. When the gun was fired to start the race all the boats planned to be as close to the line as possible, and sailing towards it as fast as possible. This advantage was lost if they were too far from it, and behind other boats. Fine judgement was required.

Before the start a lot of jockeying took place. The gun was fired exactly ten minutes before the race was due to start. Everyone had a stopwatch. This was followed by a second gun exactly five minutes later, then everyone knew to the second when they should be where they wanted to be. During these last few minutes they were gauging how fast the boat would go, and trying to guide it to the right place without clashing with any of the others.

If a boat unfortunately crossed the line before the final starting gun another gun was quickly fired and the number on the sail of the defaulter boomed out over the water from a loud hailer on the platform. This boat had to turn, go back behind the line, turn again and then follow on well behind the rest of the fleet.

I had the good fortune to be asked to crew for a boy who was about my age. His family owned a house there and also a boat. I worked the jib in the bows while he took the helm and managed the mainsail. Having spent all his holidays there he was very familiar with the area and we often won. The most help I could provide was to carry out his orders as promptly and slickly as possible, and to move swiftly to one side or the other as instructed, to balance the boat.

The property next to our house was owned by a man and his wife who spent all summer there. His boat was the largest in the club, a twenty-four foot Milne that needed four crew. Before World War Two there had been several of these boats that used to race against each other, but now his was the only one. So he could only race using an official handicap. The rest of his sailing was out to sea, fishing, when it was calm enough to supplement his larder.

As I grew older I became strong enough to become one of the crew, and after he had talked to my parents and asked permission to take me on, I had several sails. The others were grown men, on holiday like us, and their strength was needed in the stronger winds. Sometimes I brought back pollock caught by spinning, shiny hooks attached to a long line trailed behind the boat.

The skipper's great advantage was that he was very familiar with the coast of Anglesey, and its tides and currents, after the many years of sailing those waters. He knew all this in great detail, showing me charts indicating the interactions of the waters and also the positions of the underwater rocks and reefs.

Before setting off he would use these charts to plan

the day's sailing, taking note of the local weather forecast and the times of the tides. The local currents created by the ebb and flow of tides around the island were complicated.

The benefit of this knowledge was revealed when he raced. As the rest of the fleet rounded a buoy and made for the next, he would turn out to sea for a while. On reaching a fast current that he knew was there and would help him, he would turn and sail with it and arrive at the next buoy before the others – to their amazement.

One year there was a large racing regatta at Holyhead, the chief town and port of Anglesey, further north and further up the coast. There a long breakwater shelters a very large area inside it in which all classes of boats could compete around different-sized courses marked by buoys. On this occasion there were also a few very different large boats, not racing yachts, but a trawler, a ketch, a yawl and ourselves to name some. These were to sail as a special class, with suitable handicaps, and would go outside the breakwater and around a certain rock before returning.

My parents drove me there soon after breakfast and I went aboard with the crew. By this time it was fortunate that I wore an oilskin and sou'wester.

About ten o'clock we all set off, making for the end of the breakwater and the open sea. But there was a big and growing problem – steadily worsening weather. Dawn had brought heavy, dark clouds and stiff, gusting winds, and choppy seas. Now the wind was much stronger and persistent, and spume flew from the white crests of the now considerable waves. Inside the breakwater it was much calmer with only a pronounced swell, but becoming rougher around its end.

Should we, or not, risk leaving its shelter?

One by one the other boats turned back.

It was decided that it still looked possible for us so we turned to face the open sea and passed the end of the breakwater. We would take a look.

At that moment the wind hit us with terrific force. Ahead was a ferocious meeting of tides and wind, and the waves merged into gigantic cones of water that seemed to continue as far as the eye could see.

There was now no question of turning back or even tacking. Any attempt to alter course would mean being thrown over and sunk. We had to keep on through the cones. A quite terrifying sight.

After what seemed an age the cones became less pronounced, and the skipper felt it was safe to carry out a rapid tack to starboard so as to continue North parallel to the coast. We were warned to keep our heads down or be decapitated, as the mainsail boom crashed over from port to starboard. The rigging was sound and nothing parted. The sky became darker; the clouds heavier and lower. A jet plane, a Vampire, was seen streaking off the island. It turned in a wide circle and returned whence it came.

We were now in a headlong charge – the only course of action possible – that seemed to go on and on. Then, as if that wasn't bad enough, a new menace presented itself. Directly ahead appeared a huge pinnacle of rock like a cliff. Each wave broke upon it and rushed high up its smooth surface, driven by the gale, then fell down again to meet the next. As we were borne helplessly towards it the number of waves separating us from it reduced rapidly and steadily. To be wrecked upon it seemed inevitable. Nobody spoke.

When about four waves distant the wind momentarily became less, probably due to the back thrust of it from the rock, there came the sudden shouted command:

"Heads down! Right down! Tacking to starboard! "

Two waves later the helm was swung hard over, the boat turned round ninety degrees to starboard, and the boom flew to port with a mighty jar. The rock was now on our port side and we passed it rapidly, heading for the coast. A minute later another shouted command, and this time he tacked to port and we were back on our former course well past the rock.

Over the next thirty minutes or so the wind lessened a little and the sky lightened. This enabled us to yaw one hundred and eighty degrees and we were sailing South, the sea calmer, the winds steady, the sun appearing, and the helm could be lashed into a set position. We could relax at last.

Out came the beer and sandwiches. The skipper lit his pipe.

After such a harrowing and prolonged period of unremitting tension, when every moment might have been our last, there were smiles all round. Not much needed to be said, or was said, though the skipper was heartily congratulated for his skill. Eventually the conversation drifted onto topics other than sailing. Two or three hours later we returned to our mooring and rode ashore in the dinghy.

Quite a crowd lined the quay. There was clapping, and also some excited remarks of relief that we were safely back. Then into the bar where the skipper downed a 'pint-in-one', and soon he and the rest of the crew were answering a barrage of questions. The general consensus was that with his knowledge and skill he was the only man they knew who could have succeeded as he had done.

I caught sight of my parents, said my farewells, and joined them, and so home with an exciting tale to tell. They had been waiting for some time along with others, worried because we were so overdue and lost to view. The RAF jet had been dispatched to find us, coming from RAF Valley in Anglesey, and had reported seeing us sailing.

No doubt there followed much debate as to whether we should have taken the risk of going on. But "All's well that ends well" and it remains a thrilling memory. It was the last time that I went on that boat because the holiday ended, and thereafter we took our holidays later in the summer, after the sailing season had finished.

It brought home to me how lucky I was to survive, and always to be aware of what might lurk beneath an innocent-looking sea: currents, rocks and reefs, and the need to consider how quickly conditions at sea can change. Close coastal sailing should only be done by those experienced in the local complexities, with their knowledge passed on to others who wish to do the same.

FOG AND FOLLY

The occasion for this episode was when I allowed myself a rare evening off. It was early in my medical training after completing my history degree. It was in the company of three friends who had come up to Merton College, Oxford at the same time as I had. They were now studying for their doctorates and also fancied a break. One had a small Morris coupe that he serviced himself, and we drove outside Oxford to a restaurant that sold meals of the steak-and-chips and ham-egg-and-chips variety, among others.

It was a very dark, cloudy night with a lot of mist about but the visibility was reasonable and once there we enjoyed the warmth and the cheerful bright atmosphere. I emphasised the warmth because central heating was rather rare in those days, and where it existed it was much less efficient compared with that of today.

They were very busy, but it was one of my lucky nights. There was a considerable conversational din around us. I ordered a gammon steak, then just managed to hear the words "egg" and "pineapple" spoken by the waitress.

I said: "Yes, please."

There was a pause.

She said: "You mean you would like both?"

I replied: "Yes, please."

And they came – both.

Meanwhile my friends explained that I had been offered one or the other, not both. Anyway fortune shone that night!

When we emerged after one and a half hours or so the picture that greeted us was very dire. The mist had condensed into a true fog and there was no wind to disperse it. Nevertheless we had to 'make a go of it' and set off very slowly, the headlamps just able to pick out the nearside edge of the road. Luckily headlamps were not strong in those days, so there was less glare, or progress in the fog might not have been possible.

After half a mile or so – very difficult to judge in fog, in which one always seems to have travelled further than one in fact has – we came up behind the tail-lights of a lorry going very slowly.

Suddenly it pulled into the left side and rapidly came to a halt. Thinking that it may have decided to stop for a while we pulled out cautiously to overtake it. But immediately there came into view a long line of lorries parked bonnet to tail, lights still on, of which ours was the latest addition. We pulled in and waited for a good fifteen minutes.

The cause of the delay was unknown so I got out and went along the line to ascertain what was happening. I could just see across the road by the light of the headlamps, and after passing four or five lorries what I saw was horrifying.

There was a car on the grass verge parallel to the road, facing the opposite way to us. It was then that I realised with shock that the interior of the car was fully open to view. The whole of the offside of the car was missing, as though cleanly cut off by a gigantic knife: bonnet, front door, rear door and boot. The two rear seats and the passenger seat were occupied, but the driver's seat was not.

Then my gaze switched to the road and I saw a man lying on his back, his shoulders towards me, a little way back from the car. I then realised that the car must have been coming too fast, misjudged its position and struck the leading lorry, shearing off its right side. The sideways force had flung the car onto the verge and ejected the driver.

Going over to him I could see that he was alive, groaning at times, but his right leg was at an odd angle and broken well above the knee. As I bent over him I heard, with rapidly increasing alarm, the sound of a car fast approaching us from the Oxford direction. Then its lights suddenly appeared. There was no sign of it slowing and it would clearly hit us both in a second or two, or so it seemed.

Without further thought I did the only thing possible. I bent, passed my hands under his shoulders, gripped him under the armpits, then heaved him up and to the left with all my strength to a position alongside the lorry beside me. He was now protected between its front and rear wheels. He leg must have been very painful because he cried out in his dazed condition, but now it seemed more in line and at least he was safe.

A car flashed past. Now realising that something was very wrong the brakes were being applied very hard, and it drew up someway further on. Its speed must have been as reckless in those conditions as that of the wrecked car.

There was nothing more I could do so I went back to my friends and explained. It was many years before the age of mobile phones, so we eased out and crept on past the carnage. The sheared-off parts of the car lay scattered along the road behind it.

We had just left it all behind when there came to us the welcome sound of a siren, and soon blue lights were dimly seen. It was a very rural road but someone must have found a house and a 'phone and called an ambulance.

The fog thinned a little as we reached the city; the street lamps helped and we reached safety. I assume that the driver would have made a full recovery.

The whole experience brought home to us the danger of driving in mist or fog and the difficulty of assessing distance travelled. If caught in either the answer is to stop, or if it is possible to proceed to do so with extreme caution, not expecting to be where we think we might be but to wait for some positive recognition. Caution all the way!

IT'S NOT ALL SUNSHINE …

"Going on holiday." What that phrase conjures up! Different things for different people.

For most it brings an uplift of mood, and air of excitement, and pleasure in anticipation. These feelings quicken as the time approaches. It is something to look forward to and to plan for.

In essence it means a complete break from routine. Pleasing oneself. Doing what one wants to do rather than what is required to be done.

Different things for different people.

Children are excited. It means a total change from the known (school, home and its environment) to the unknown, with all its possibilities. They will be exploring new areas or revisiting old ones that, by familiarity, have come to embody the very idea and meaning of 'holiday'. Not having to plan the packing, journey, meals and money their vision is of an unbroken bout of self-indulgence.

Adults, of course, have to do all the planning and preparation: an unwanted burden after being wearied by a long spell of work and home routines? Not so! The very thought of holiday is refreshing in itself. To quote the old adage – 'a change is as good as a rest'.

It gets one out of a rut. The prospect of enjoyment seems to bring out the energy that you never knew you had. The nearer it comes the time seems to drag, each day longer than the one before – especially for children.

Once a holiday has begun the time seems to fly by, and all too soon it will be over. The length of it may make a difference. If a short one of a very few days there is an acute awareness that time is limited, and there is a determination to 'make use of every minute'. The 'short break' can be very satisfying.

The mistake with a longer one is to let the first few days drift by before 'getting into gear' and doing meaningful things. Sad realisation that they seem to have been wasted can taint the time that remains. The secret is to do at least something considered worthwhile early on.

Of course there are those who intend to have a relaxing and lazy time throughout, and nothing more.

Different things for different people.

Do holidays live up to expectation? Looking back on them is never as quite as enjoyable as looking forward to them. After all, they are now over. Family occasions with children, the pursuits being pretty repetitive, can become a blurred though happy memory as time goes by –

though hard to recall what happened on what day. Beforehand, the hope that was 'top-of-the-list' was for a plentiful combination of sun and beach at home or abroad. But before the advent of climate change – apart from some exceptional years – the reality at home was mostly dull days, cloud, wind and rain, real or threatening. If one really pleasant hot day occurred it was felt that it had been worth waiting for, and that this essential had brought fulfilment for the holiday. Once total immersion in the cold sea had been braved one felt warmer in than out.

Yet there was a great deal to be said for bracing weather, and it had to be experienced before this was appreciated: walking along cliff tops, scrambling over rocks and searching rock pools, and being drenched by spray as large rollers crashed against the coast some yards away. This unusual feeling of invigoration outdoors was enjoyable, and then, on going indoors, it quickly gave way to complete and relaxed lassitude, almost sleepiness – and a large appetite. All very satisfying!

At home such conditions would only have urged a retreat indoors at the earliest possible moment.

Nowadays, since climate change has taken a hold, there may be not one but a succession of days and nights that are long and hot and uncomfortable. People discover that the heat generated by any activity will not be off-loaded to the surrounding air. They become overheated and their energy 'sapped'. This new and extreme situation, which at first might seem to hold such promise for a holiday, rather puts an damper on a desire to do anything much. Oh for a happy medium that never seems to happen!

Whatever one's intentions the general conduct and activities of a holiday tend to be governed by the conditions in which it takes place. So looking back the whole can become a blur of 'much of the same', and then it is often the case that odd and totally unexpected events are seen as the highlights of the holiday. And these are talked about years later, when all the rest of the detail has been forgotten.

"Do you remember the time when …?", and so on.

There spring to mind a few such events when on a six week holiday with friends in Italy in 1960. The overall impression remains of a relentless, burning sun by day, miles of tramping over hot, dusty ground, the need for copious water, and nights warm enough to lie without tents under the stars.

But a misfortune befell me as we travelled by train to Italy via France and Switzerland. Queuing to go on the Metro to the south of Paris I had to keep bending to lower my valise (containing everything needed for six weeks) to the floor, then doing the same to pick it up as the queue moved slowly forward. Suddenly the seam in the seat of my trousers gave way leaving a wide gap. So began a twenty-four hour challenge to try and minimise pants exposure, and in which we took in a tour of Milan Cathedral. Luckily we sat up all night in a carriage. I had a needle and thread, but the first chance to strip and repair did not occur until on our campsite above Florence. Inexpert I might be but I made very sure it would hold. Not an episode to forget!

This campsite was situated well above Florence, a long slope of short grass studded with sizeable olive trees. One night we awoke suddenly about 3am, all immediately sensing that the heavens were about to open. It's curious that one does so intuitively. Hastily we gathered our things together and ran for the only cover available, the thick green plastic surround to several wash basins. Enormous drops began to fall as we arrived and crouched underneath.

For the next two hours our senses were battered by a thunderstorm of an intensity that I have never experienced since. The heavy, dense, forceful rain deafened us by hammering on the green plastic like a drum. The lightening flashed continuously. At some time most will have experienced thunder directly overhead, sounding as though the furniture is being thrown about upstairs – quite terrifying. Over Florence it lasted for two whole hours.

It stopped as suddenly as it began, the rumbles dying away rapidly and the rain stopping as if a tap had been turned off. Fearing the possibility of more, and the ground being wet, we stayed where we were until, after the sun was up, we emerged stiff and aching to find the ground hard and dry as though it had never happened.

A similar nocturnal storm was the only other time it rained during the six weeks.

Another surprise came a few days later when we were bedded down in a field by a hedge high in the hills around Sienna. Lying on my side, with my eyes about to close, I suddenly perceived a small cloud of pin-pricks of light among the grasses nearby. I blinked, but there was no doubt. What could it be? 'Fairies at the bottom of the garden' sprang to mind. I called out and someone turned and said it was fireflies – he being an habitual camper in the wild. This was my first and only sight of them. Perhaps I should sleep more under the stars. They formed an entrancing spectacle.

The thunderstorm had been a massive assault on the senses, but a mental shock awaited us when the veneer of civilised behaviour, with which Italy had impressed us, was suddenly cracked by no less a responsible citizen than the stationmaster at Pompeii.

We had been most impressed by the Italian railway system. It was fully electrified and ran exactly to time. The stations were clean and new (rebuilt after the war), and for travellers' convenience a board carried a representation of the make-up of the next train due to arrive. Between the engine and guard's van the carriages and trucks were arranged in order so that passengers could work out where to wait on the platform to get on.

Our train arrived at Pompeii where there was an hour's wait until the next connection. Directly opposite the station was the ancient city covered in pumice, then only just starting to be excavated. It was too good an opportunity to miss, but our bags were too heavy to carry while we explored it.

There were only one or two other passengers waiting. The waiting room and stationmaster's office were glass-walled from floor to roof and connected by a door. The stationmaster was behind his desk. He did not speak English but understood enough to indicate that we could leave our bags in the waiting room, easily visible to him.

There was only time for a rapid look round, going through the old gateway where the Roman carts had worn two deep ruts in the stone base, and exploring the paved main street that stretched straight ahead. The windows and doors of the terraced houses on either side opened onto a pavement raised above road level, a stepping-stone in front of each door to ease connection with the street. Some houses had internal coloured murals.

Returning to the station in good time for the train we were aghast. Our bags had disappeared. Then they were seen lined up behind the stationmaster – perhaps he was kindly keeping them safe. As we went forward to his office he looked stern, raised his hand, and stopped us at the door. Clearly he wanted money to release them!

In exasperation we went into the square outside and managed to persuade a member of the carabinieri – a sort of policeman in a light khaki uniform and carrying a rifle – to come with us to the station. Unfortunately he spoke no English and seemed in awe of the stationmaster, who was very firm with him. Back to the square! This time a man who had been watching our efforts came across to us. In a belted raincoat and soft hat, and with an air of authority, he looked like a plain-clothes policeman. He spoke good English and asked what the problem was. We explained.

He took us to the station and ordered that our bags be released to us. He smiled and said "it will be all right now", and left. I wish that he had stayed! Before returning our bags the stationmaster insisted on filling in a form for each of us, many questions to be answered (name, address, family details etc. etc.) so making us miss our train despite our protests. We had to catch a later one.

Had we been older and more experienced I think we would have simply taken the bags and ignored him. It was staggering to think that this sort of Mafia-effect should be practised so directly on tourists fifteen years after the war had ended. Tourism was so important to the local economy, and it was not all that far south. It was a relief to move on and away from a scene of such unpleasantry.

Four years later I travelled through Germany to Yugoslavia (at the time still one country) and Greece. Looking back it was very enjoyable, but a great deal of driving – we all took turns – and again it was very hot throughout.

I recall a minor incident just as we crossed the very high mountains from Austria into Northern Yugoslavia. I put a hand into my jacket inside pocket and it emerged covered in ink. In those days before biros became the universal writing tool I took with me a fountain pen to write postcards. At that height above sea-level the air in the pen's rubber reservoir had expanded and forced the ink to leak out. A lesson for the return journey!

Descending from the mountains we drove southwest to make our evening camp on the shore of the rocky Adriatic, passing through scenery as delightful as the Austrian Tyrol to the north: wooden chalets with huge overhanging eaves and window boxes full of flowers, predominantly red. Passing through a fir wood, with less than a mile to the sea, we passed a herd of goats minded by a girl of about seven and a brother half that age. We paused while the way was cleared, then the girl jumped on our running board and asked in perfect English where we were going. She was excited about the idea of camping, gave her brother stern instructions to stay with the goats and insisted on coming to see what we did. She stayed on the running board.

She was fascinated. The surprise was the excellence of her English, then taught as the second language in that country. Never before had she seen lilos – we did not have tents. Our evening meals were cooked in a large bowl on a gas primus stove, and into it we put potatoes and vegetables bought on the way, and meat from a tin. This not being cattle country we brought all the meat needed in the car in tins.

At this point it was considered best to return a very reluctant girl to her brother, by driving her back. But before she went she insisted on writing down all our names and addresses on paper that we lent her, and to our further amazement she wrote everything down in beautifully executed copperplate script.

Likewise Greece was rather a marathon drive: heat, dust and the constant glare of the windscreen off the white, dusty roads. But it was full of general interest: the mountains in the north, cuckoo-house monasteries perched on basalt columns in the northwest, the frenetic traffic in Athens, and the original site of the Olympic Games in the undulating Peloponnese. Our favourite place was Delphi. Spending so long exploring the ancient temples we had to camp just above the ruins on a steep, sloping hillside from where we had a distant view of the Gulf of Corinth. As we lay in a row with a very starry sky above and distant music sounding from the town below, two men in large sombrero-type hats came walking up the hill towards us, clearly Spanish and in a merry mood, each carrying a large gourd of wine with a pipe protruding – like a bagpipe.

They greeted us cheerfully, spoke no English, but indicated by mime that we should keep still and open our mouths. This we did, immediately a jet of wine was squirted from the pipes into each of our mouths – just the right amount so as not to overfill – and not a drop spilt anywhere. Then, with a cheerful farewell, they went on their way. I had heard of this Spanish skill but never expected to come across it, least of all in Greece.

The final highlight of our holiday was so unexpected and so touching that it brought a warm glow when we were treated to some Greek hospitality for which that country is renowned.

Crossing to the island of Zakynthos, on the western side of the country, the ferry being an old tank-landing craft from the war, we worked our way to the southern end – it not being at all developed for tourists as it is now. Each signpost had a name of a place in Greek letters but at the next intersection the name would not be repeated but different, and so on, so we never arrived 'anywhere'. But at the very end of the island was an old, rusted derrick and patches of hardened oil where drilling for oil must once have been attempted.

Near it was a single-story cottage, a large tree fifty yards from it, and underneath its spreading branches a rough wooden table and benches. We parked and looked about. At that moment a wiry man, short in stature with a face wizened by the sun, came over to us. One of us knew some Greek and managed to explain our presence.

Once they knew that we were on holiday and English he became very pleased and friendly, and insisted that we sit down at the table where he plied us with wine, salad, and some meats and bread. It was quite a meal. His wife peered at us from the doorway a few times, for she had prepared the food, but never showed any sign of coming over.

Eventually we left, very much to his regret, and from his effusive handshaking and show of comradeship it would seem that we had quite made his day. No money would be taken of course.

Our holiday was drawing to a close, and with a happy ending that we would always treasure, a fitting finale that holidays never usually have.

A GP IN OXFORD

The Return to Oxford

Carole and I came back to Oxford in September, 1977, with two small sons. A daughter was to be born the next year. We had spent the first six years of our married life "On Station" in the RAF, three of them in West Germany, the whole experience being interesting, socially enjoyable, and at times exciting. My work had been that of a GP (for families as well as Personnel) but with additional aspects to do with flying, for which special training had been given. An extra duty for my final year was to lecture pilots on the medical angles related to flying, to refresh their memories as they retrained to fly new types of aircraft. All this came in useful later in civilian practise.

The next one-and-three-quarter years were spent as a civilian GP in Worcester, where at last I could be a doctor to patients over fifty-five years of age! I was able to take part in the new national scheme whereby the GP formed a "team" with the midwife to take part with her in the delivery of babies, as well as running the Ante- and Post-Natal clinics. I had prepared for this by working in the obstetric unit of the RAF hospital in West Germany for the requisite six months, and then taken the Diploma in Obstetrics with the Royal College of Obstetricians and Gynaecologists.

We lived in Pershore, ten miles from Worcester. Our house was on high ground and looked across the Vale of Evesham to Bredon Hill in the distance, an outcrop of the Cotswolds. It would be hard to discover a more idyllic view. Miles of fields and orchards stretched away until the Hill, with several villages around its base, reared up as a back drop.

Unfortunately, working in Worcester became unsatisfactory for various reasons, and more so as time went on. Also the city had lost the charm of its ancient centre through demolition – which is why we did not live there – and an ugly muddle of roads and buildings had partially replaced it. The question was where to move to!

Oxford was our number one choice. Carole was happy to return to where she was brought up, her close family living there or nearby. I looked upon Oxford and Merton College as "Home", having lived there continuously for more than ten years – longer than in any other place: History Degree, eight months converting to science, Degrees in Medicine and Surgery, and my first "House

Job" after qualifying. The second had been in Birmingham. Also I had had the opportunity to become familiar with many areas of non-university Oxford, over five years, through Carole, her family and friends until being married in 1970 and going off on active service.

Trying to find a Practice vacancy in Oxford from a distance was all but impossible in those days because Practices there tended not to advertise. What counted was knowing people and "word of mouth". I contacted my former GP from Merton and through him discovered that not his, but another practice in the same building, was looking for a new partner – and luck was on my side!

Unusual Appeal of the Practice

The attractions of the new practice made it unique in Oxford: the large spread of the practice area, and the variety of our work.

Different areas of Oxford have very different social structures. Most surgeries have small practice areas, being situated where the population density is adequate for a Practice List. But the permanent resident population around my new Practice in the city centre was relatively small, and so to gain sufficient numbers our area had to encompass most of Oxford, with all its variety, as far as was practicable. Distance and traffic congestion were the main determining factors – how long it would take to make domiciliary visits. We did not cover certain outlying areas in North and East Oxford that were too far and away and too difficult to get to, and which were anyway adequately served by their local Practices.

However, we were able to accept back from these areas patients who had been moved there when the dilapidated housing of the central St. Ebbes district was demolished in the 1970s. They had been a real community, and when the new housing was complete (this time with main drainage!) a large number returned.

It was with rather a sad feeling that I used to visit an old bed-ridden lady at the top of the last house left standing in this area. All around it was a scene of brick-strewn, flattened desolation in which the former pattern of the streets could be discerned. She had lived there all her life and refused to move. The rest of the building was empty but the Council kindly left her there in peace to see out her days, and these turned out to be few in number.

Our equal involvement with all ranges of society was a truly Chaucerian experience. As well as University Colleges we covered a number of other academic institutions teaching English to foreign students, Media and Business Studies, A and O levels and Diplomas. I became official doctor to the Oxford Centre for Islamic Studies, and for many years was the honorary advisor to the Allergy Support Group.

The practice had several private assignments. We were medical advisors to the OUP, dealing with 'on site' emergencies and medical assessment for future employees. Also medical assessments for underwater divers who examined bridges, dams etc. for Thames Water. Various hotels used us for emergencies. I remember a patient from Eastern Europe producing a bundle of currency notes the size of a nearly – complete toilet roll, wrapped in elastic bands, and peeled off the required amount. For a while I carried out a lunchtime emergency clinic at Selfridges.

We took many patients from South and West Oxford and their outlying areas.

We served a very large Asian population, mostly from East and South Oxford. Many first-generation women did not speak English, but their children were the best translators, their husbands finding it difficult to mention 'women's problems' and their vocabulary was limited. These families coped by living in a close community, providing mutual support. We would write supportive letters to the Council to advise that new arrivals be housed as near to the established groups as possible.

There was also a considerable amount of less congenial work that no other practice wanted: various hostels and police surgeon duties.

The hostels housed men and women who had been homeless, were social misfits or incapable of managing on their own. Many were from psychiatric units and judged well-enough to be released to a "Half-way House". A significant number needed to be readmitted to the Littlemore or the Warneford Hospitals when problems came to a head and their condition reverted – often in the "Early Hours!". Many others had a "grey area" personality disorder, but not a treatable psychiatric condition. Some event would trigger an episode of bizarre behaviour or of considerable social disturbance with threatening verbal abuse and violence. Admission to a police cell was sometimes the only answer until they calmed down. Sometimes such people could be taken there by the police in the first instance to remove them from somewhere in the public arena, calling us because it was assumed they had a psychiatric problem.

A visit to the hostel for homeless teenagers was always a desperately sad affair. They were fleeing from broken homes or had been ejected from them and were "passing through". They were allowed to stay for the evening and night only and then had to move on.

Finally there was the Night Shelter for the homeless and alcoholics. They had medical care by day from a part-time doctor in a portakabin next door (now a brick building), but we were "on call" for them at nights and weekends.

No one else wanted to take on the police work.

The Police Work

This was a heavy workload for the doctor "on call" and on the whole rather unpleasant, but it paid well, which is why we did it. There were usually several calls, day and night, often to several prisoners at a time, and on arrival we would often find that more cases had been added at one or both Oxford police stations – all very time-consuming.

The police were obliged to call us if a prisoner asked to see a doctor. They also called us for reasons of their own: to assess injuries to prisoners or police officers, prisoners' mental health and to assess 'fitness to drive'! If the Breathalyser showed the Blood Alcohol level to be just over the legal limit the prisoners were offered the chance to have a blood test that might show the level to be just below the legal limit.

Prisoners were not always grateful or polite when the doctor came at their request. One was deep asleep when I arrived in the depths of the night. On being woken he looked at me with bleary eyes then said that now that he had seen me I could go, and anyway I was **** ugly. He turned over and went back to sleep.

Women police officers from a specially-trained team assisted in the examination of alleged victims of rape, in a specially-equipped building far from the station. These lengthy procedures – maybe three or four hours – often took place during the night, leaving little time to go home and prepare to reach the surgery for 7.30am, and get ready for the 8.00am clinic to start.

We were called to all cases of unexpected deaths, where the GP was unknown or could not come. Even if it seemed obvious the police were never allowed to assume that death had occurred. I recall a railway suicide where the officer present carefully indicated the three separate locations of the body, head and brain "In case it's of any help, Doc!" Another case was entangled in the front wheels of a diesel locomotive, clearly beyond recovery to the most untrained eye, but I had to reach it in the early hours of a very frosty morning, stepping from one very slippery railway sleeper to another, the distance between them inconveniently longer that a normal stride. The huge stones between them were large, sharp and would ruin any footwear except very tough boots. Seeing this engine from the track level made it seem so much bigger that from the platform and so powerful, the ground shaking as the motor throbbed in neutral.

A good example of never simply assuming death to have occurred was that of a man who had collapsed in an outside toilet and been observed not to move for a long time. The officer apologised for having to call a doctor when he was so clearly dead. In fact there was a heartbeat and the man was taken to hospital, though he died later.

The really unpleasant cases were suicide by hanging, often in the gloom of the "Early Hours", whether from a bridge, from the bannisters in a hallway, or even from the hook behind the bedroom door where the dressing gown would usually hang. A rather strange case was that of a man who had dressed very neatly in his 'Sunday Best', with shoes polished, hair brushed tidily and a carefully-written note explaining everything and apologising to all involved.

Working with a uniformed branch was a happy reminder of my time with the RAF – their discipline, their pride in what is done, and the worth of good sergeants. Good humour was very evident and so essential considering that the police deal with all those sides of life that people don't want to experience – violence, drink and drug problems and unpleasant situations arising from disturbed personalities.

The police called us "Doc" (easier than remembering a name) but I think they liked this familiarity because it made them feel we were part of their team. In reality we were strictly independent and neutral. They may be convinced that someone is unfit to drive, and usually they were right, but on the occasions when we said that this was not so they had to go along with this although they sometimes looked most incredulous. Reports had to be submitted to solicitors on request over any type of case. At times we had to appear in courts in cases we had been personally involved with, as expert medical witnesses. It was with a deep sense of satisfaction that in certain notable cases I was able to promote the cause of justice by thwarting a barrister's attempts to discredit me as a witness. When barristers were in difficulties they tended to bluster and ask rather outrageous questions. I remember one particular one in whose left cheek an obvious twitch developed immediately before he delivered one of his more disagreeable questions.

On a more pleasant note we had to conduct a medical examination of all recruits applying to join the Thames Valley Police Force. Various sites were used but eventually a permanent location was established at a police training college near Reading. It was a pleasant relief from routine work to drive past Wallingford to this beautiful estate with excellent views, and carry out the work in a grand old country house with a huge pillared portico and a maze of "back stairs" that led to the rooms that we used. We were even given a mug of tea! It was of great interest to chat to the recruits and discover how varied their backgrounds and their reasons for applying were.

The University

When I joined the practice we covered seven colleges, (Christchurch, Magdalen, Worcester, Wadham, Keeble,

Hertford, New College, and later Regents Park), though sadly not Merton. It was always a pleasure to visit them for domiciliary visits, especially in the sunshine of the spring and summer. I enjoyed being involved with University life once more and found it very useful that I was able to appreciate what kind of working lives both Arts and Science students had to lead: both because I had been among them when "Up" for so many years, but also because I had read subjects on both sides. At times I found it helpful to inform troubled students of this, and it was with immediate and evident relief that they realised that I understood what they were up against. We were on the same wavelength.

Another enjoyable task was to assist the Medical School by taking in Pre-clinical and Clinical Medical students for several weeks at a time to familiarise them with clinical medicine and surgery in all its aspects as far as GP practice was concerned; also to pass on so much that one has worked out for oneself over the years and which is never found in books or clinical teaching.

Equally interesting was having Senior Members of the University as patients, and the opportunity to appreciate how much their lives were coloured, not only by teaching and research, but also by other very real College concerns and problems.

I was a GP in Oxford for twenty-five years. The Senior Partner had been the official doctor to all the Colleges, but when he retired in 1985 he managed to persuade them to have the rest of the Partners as College doctors, each being appointed to one or more Colleges. Wadham kindly agreed to accept me and I enjoyed seventeen years of getting to know the fellows well, "Dining In" once a week in Term (over four hundred dinners in all). It was at their request "to keep in touch," though of course my dealings with students as patients were entirely confidential and never discussed.

I recall many a jolly evening as conversation flowed, spiced at times by the presence of guests from home or abroad, academic or otherwise. Of those graduates or senior academics who came to Wadham for up to three years I remember among others a Chinese man from Xiang whose project was "Love in the English Novel"; a French Professor with a great sense of humour who was most informative about French wines and the soils in which they grew; and a German Lektor (History) who was winning great accolades in Germany and who got through prodigious amounts of work. I was sorry when they left.

I must not leave High Table without mentioning Keeley, a retired physicist in his nineties who still lived in the College. Being rather deaf in one ear people tended not to sit next to him but I always sought to do so (on whichever side) because I enjoyed his company. Kindly and courteous he had a fund of interesting stories to tell, and interesting small scientific instruments that he would produce from his waistcoat and jacket pockets and demonstrate between courses. He had been put in charge of the Clarendon Laboratory in World War Two, Lord Cherwell being otherwise occupied. He described a rather frightening experience when he went up in an aircraft at the Farnborough Aerodrome where experimentation was carried out. A method had been worked out to get an aircraft out of an invariably fatal spin. The plane was put into a clockwise spin, Keeley sitting in the aircraft taking notes, and the technique worked. Thinking that that was the end of the matter Keeley was horrified when it was decided that this should also work for an anticlockwise spin and that this should be put to the test. It worked. He professed to deep feelings of triumph, but also of relief!

At the start of each academic year, in "Noughth Week", I had to lecture to the "Freshers" for ten minutes or so, explaining about the medical services offered by our surgery and to present a friendly and approachable face. This took place in the Holywell Music Room with its wonderful acoustics. I was one of a succession of speakers and always followed the Domestic Bursar, often a retired senior naval officer at Wadham. I recall one of them who always stood very erect with his hands behind his back, and out of habit spoke to them as though he were addressing the Ship's Company. I'm sure that they felt that I would follow with information about the Sick Bay on board, but I had to bring them back rapidly to Oxford and land-based civilian life.

Reflections on changes over twenty-five years

As the years went by the most obvious change was the ever-increasing workload. Both patients and practice partners increased in number. Each day we would add extra patients to already-full lists, fitting them in, and learning to speed up consultations although conducting them as satisfactorily as ever. Two of us always began clinics at 8am to see those who wanted to avoid missing work. The police work increased hugely, and to prevent exhaustion for the "on call" doctor the weekend "on call" was reduced from seventy-two to forty-eight hours. There was never a day or half-day off after being "on call", even after weekends.

There was an obvious answer to the increasing workload: an appropriate increase in the numbers of doctors and staff, and at the same time everyone "went the extra mile" to get things done – an approach mirrored by the hospitals. Each practice could decide on its own enlargement in consultation with the local health authority.

But the point came when more doctors and staff were needed than were officially permitted – the limit being due to cost. So then governments approached the problem from the wrong angle, saying that doctors need not work at nights or weekends if they did not want to, thus being more rested. Agencies would provide locum doctors to replace them for those sessions.

This produced two problems. First, by substituting one doctor for another they did not provide the increase in doctor or staff numbers that was needed, and the increasing patient workload was not going to go away. The second sequel was that the locums had no access to patient notes and so did not know the medical history of the patient. Patients can be very vague about their medical past and may be old, rather deaf or poorly-sighted, and often nervous with a strange doctor – especially if foreign, and then invariably with a limited vocabulary. The upshot was that the regular doctors had to deal with these cases as an added burden when they returned to work, starting very much from scratch. The practice continuity of care was broken, and the workload unnecessarily heavier.

As for the police work it was the change in the type of case seen in the Custody Suit that stood out. Whereas the main nuisances in the early years were older men and women and alcoholism, they gradually became greatly outnumbered by young men and women (mostly teenagers) who were addicted to drugs or sniffed glue. They create a public nuisance, thieve to be able to buy their expensive drugs, and are caught buying, selling or using them. They are usually arrogant, lying, demanding and abusive: most unpleasant to deal with. Dealing with their withdrawal symptoms when in custody was a major task. They could not be sent to hospital as an in-patient because the hospitals had neither the room nor the staff to spare to deal with them, and being under arrest each one would have to be accompanied by a policeman: again, none to spare for this purpose.

Another marked change was the increase in local violence – in common with other cities – and the emergence of more gang culture than before. The streets were no longer so safe at night and sometimes the same could be said of them by day. Drugs, alcohol and family break-up counted for a lot of this, and the plethora of wine bars and clubs that sprang up, often staying open until the early hours, did not help.

A great mistake was the attempt to put all patients' notes on computer, instead of using the written notes system, to make hospitals and GP's surgeries "paperless". The idea was that if a patient consulted a doctor anywhere in the country the notes would be accessed instantly. This, the most expensive computer scheme in Europe, was designed to cater for those moving about the UK, but it is relatively rarely that people attend surgeries other than their own, even on holiday. If necessary their own surgery could easily be contacted for information. The project ran into insurmountable difficulties and had to be abandoned.

If only doctors had been widely consulted about the whole idea it would have been 'dead in the water' from the outset. Trying to put adequate medical information of this type onto a computer is not practical. For decades doctors have been trained to make notes on consultations in the same way, often with labelled diagrams, that are readily understood by any doctor that sees them. These are made very quickly, either during a consultation or immediately afterwards, while the evidence is fresh in the doctor's mind.

This simply cannot be put on the computer in the desired arrangement that is made on paper, and using the computer is time-consuming. To look at any computer printout shows how meagre and inadequate the record is. The sparse facts have no "colour".

The other major point is that the use of the computer completely disrupts a consultation. It should be a continuous engagement with the patient from the time that the room is entered: conversation, examination, explanation of results and planned treatment, if any. To keep turning away and pressing keys is an unacceptable break in contact. If the doctor waits until the end of the whole surgery to address the computer it is difficult to recall all the necessary detail, and doctors have taken literally hours trying to keep the computer records up to date.

There is also the danger of losing patient confidentiality due to hacking (even the Pentagon is not immune) or by transferring such information to the wrong place accidentally – as has been done. The written records kept in the surgery are much safer.

These major errors have a common starting point.

It is the usual one of the Department of Health asking bureaucracy to implement ideas, the bureaucrats not being medically trained and having no true concept of how medical matters should be handled. A sad corollary to this has been the prevention of one aspect of the close cooperation of GPs and consultants, important for the patients' best interests. If a patient does not need to attend A&E but should be seen by a certain clinic within twenty-four hours or so, a consultant or the registrar would add that patient to that clinic the next day after a chat and explanation by the GP. This was no longer allowed. It was bureaucracy that was to decide the length of the clinics and the consultants were not allowed to "run their own shows". All they could do was apologise, say that their hands were tied, and could only advise that the patient be sent to A&E. This department was then flooded with patients that should not be there, and it takes hours and hours for harassed junior doctors there (less experienced than the GP) to eventually steer them to where the GP wanted to send them in the first place.

GP surgeries and hospitals fully 'manned', seven days

and nights a week, is the obvious answer, adding to patient safety at weekends and preventing the weekend problems being added to the weekday load. No wonder morale and recruitment are so poor. It takes years and money to recruit and train up medical staff of every variety, so there is no quick fix. The drive to do this should be planned, explained to the country at large, and started now. This would at least give people more understanding about the present difficulties and give everyone hope, and a sense of purpose to work towards this future goal, aware that at last things will get better. It is the only way.

JUSTICE

It was a very dark night. Starless. A heavy storm smote and drenched the farmhouse and the brick barns and outbuildings of the adjacent farmyard. Rain bounced off the concrete that covered the yard, then ran as little runnels onto the two tracks leading out of it, and so to the fields. Earth soon became thick, glutinous mud.

Within the farmhouse the open fire burned brightly, but the rain reached even here, the drops hissing now and again as they fell down the broad chimney and fell prey to the flames. The farmer and his wife could hear the water on the windows and the wind moaning around the eaves and through the twists and turns of the yard by the house. This was all background noise to the warm haven of peace within.

Then slowly they became aware of occasional sounds that were very indistinct, but at odds with what would be expected in a gale. They seemed to come from the yard itself, beyond the curtained window that overlooked it. It was no weather to investigate outside, and anything seen through that window would be a blur, and the room's light would impair night vision. Besides which they felt rather vulnerable alone in the house. A sixth sense was operating.

"Stay here Betty, and don't draw the curtains. I'll go upstairs and peer from the bedroom window – maybe even open it. It's sheltered by the overhang. I think that it's best not to put on the outside lights until I see what is happening."

Betty looked anxious, and watched her husband rise and go up the stairs. She heard him go into the bedroom.

It seemed no time at all before he was down again, this time much more quickly.

"Well, Colin?" She asked, worry all too evident in her voice.

"I can't see anything very clearly, but I am sure that there are shadows moving by the barns where the livestock are. Of course, they are locked in, but if there is any rustling taking place we can't deal with it on our own. They may play rough. We'll keep the light on as it is, so that we seem unaware of anything happening. I'll ring Jim and Alex to stand by." These were the dairyman and the tractor driver who lived in cottages down the lane, the only exit from the farm to the main road.

"Now I'll phone the police," said Colin, and went into the hall. Betty could hear his voice, though not what he said. She decided to prepare herself for whatever might happen, and put on boots and a mac and waterproof hat from the scullery by the kitchen.

Colin came back. The police would be here in fifteen minutes or so, in force, in an incident van. Jim and Alex would see them arrive and follow after them. He then went to the scullery and donned his boots, oilskin and sou'wester. Then they both retreated to the hall window and peered into the gloom with the light out. They felt nervous and more tense as the minutes went by.

Suddenly they sensed movement outside – figures coming up the lane. The police must have left the van by the gate. And Jim and Alex would have joined them and explained the layout of the farm. They hastened to the front door, opened it, went into the open porch and closed it behind them.

Going forward to the lane they met the policemen, seven in all, and had a hurried conference with the sergeant. Colin explained about the outside light. Three men were sent round the house to watch the entrance to the yard on the other side. One was to remain at the entrance by the front of the house.

"Turn the outside lights on now," said the sergeant, "then we'll move in."

Twenty seconds later the lights came on. Unnoticed before, a large cattle lorry stood outside the yard.

One barn door stood open, and sheep were slowly emerging, shepherded out by a man behind them. Three more men stood near the barn. The door to the pigsty stood open, but the pigs could be heard inside.

Startled and blinded by the sudden light two men were seized and handcuffed before they could move, but the third reacted quickly and ran very fast towards the lorry. The policemen at the entrance did the only thing possible and brought him down hard in the mud with a rugby tackle, and sat on his back bending one arm up towards his shoulder. One of the constables from the far entrance came and applied the handcuffs, and they stood him up. The rustler hemmed in by the sheep had no option but to surrender.

The police van was fetched by the driver and in ten minutes all four rustlers were locked in it under guard. Another constable was detailed to drive the cattle lorry.

Colin and Betty thanked the sergeant for saving their livestock and coming so quickly.

"That's what we're here for," he replied. "There's far too much of this going on at the moment, and it's always a gang to herd the animals into a lorry. So we came in force, as I said on the 'phone. We'll be off to the station now, so please go back inside." The vehicles drove off into the night.

Jim and Alex had moved the sheep back into the barn, and closed the pigsty door, and they now joined Betty and Colin in the farmhouse for a 'thank-you' and a celebratory nightcap – but in the kitchen, because of muddy boots. Then they left for home.

"In future I shall leave those outside lights on all night, every night, to deter any future attempts," said Colin to Betty.

Later that night there was a request for the police surgeon to attend the police station in the town near the farm. The doctor "on call" for a certain practice there also acted as police surgeon if required for this purpose. It was still a filthy night and he became soaked as he walked from his car into the station, hefting his heavy black bag. After climbing the stairs to the third floor he entered the Custody Suite with its familiar odours. The sergeant met him and explained that a man who had been arrested in a farmyard that night was complaining of pain in his head, so would he be kind enough to examine him.

Taking him along to a cell he unlocked the door, left it open, and the doctor went in. A very thin, surly-looking man was sitting on the solid fixed concrete structure, along one side-wall, that was topped with thick, fixed wooden boards. It served as a chair or bed. Blankets were folded on it behind him, ready for use.

"Here's the doctor to see you," said the sergeant.

"I'm told that you have pain in your head," said the doctor. "Where is the pain?"

The man did not move. But continued to look surly,

"It's important that you show me where the pain is,"

explained the doctor, "or I won't know where to examine you."

After a pause the man said nothing, and quickly touched his left ear.

"What caused your pain?" asked the doctor, but receiving no reply he realised that there was not going to be any further communication so he proceeded to examine the whole of the head, ears, eyes, nose and mouth, and all the head and jaw movements. The man cooperated on request, but still said nothing. The doctor straightened, closed his bag, and said: "I am unable to find anything wrong with you on examination, and since you won't tell me anything to guide me I am unable to do any more for now. I am going back to the sergeant to report."

Leaving the cell he closed the self-locking door behind him and detailed the recent scene to the sergeant. He filled in his official notes, and then the administrative entries for the sergeant, who thanked him for coming. He then wended his wet and weary way back home.

It was some months later that the same doctor received a summons to attend the Crown Court in the town, on a certain date, as an expert medical witness in the case of '… vs. the … Police Force'! The name was that of the man that he had examined with the supposed pain in his head. On enquiry, the man was charging the police with assault by holding him down on the ground at the farmyard and hammering a round metal bar, flat at both ends, into his left ear that was uppermost at the time.

The night before he was due to attend court the doctor was "on-call" and visiting the police station to see some cases. As he was chatting to the sergeant afterwards, the latter said: "I understand that you are going to Crown Court tomorrow for the head injury case. It has been in session for the last two days, and the prosecuting barrister is ruling the roost so far. He manages to discredit the witnesses that the police bring forward, including two ENT surgeons, one on each day. He's very fiery and aggressive, apparently. I don't envy you tomorrow Doc!"

Going home, the doctor felt very uneasy. Usually the police surgeon appears in a case when the police are prosecuting, and on these occasions the prosecuting counsel leads the doctor helpfully through his evidence. Then the defending counsel rises to his feet and tries to discredit the doctor's evidence, an unpleasant experience.

This time it was to be the other way round. How could the opinion of not one, but two ENT consultants, be discredited? Of course, he did not know what had been said in there in the last two days, but the story unnerved him.

Reading up his notes the next day, before attending court, he could not find anything to concern him. He felt very tense and worried indeed when he entered the open area outside the court rooms shortly after 9am the next day. Luckily he had managed some sleep. Business in the court started routinely at 10am.

He hadn't been sitting long on one of the padded benches around the large hall when an usher in a black cloak walked towards him.

"Dr Roberts?"

"Yes."

"The defending counsel would very much like to see you for a few minutes before the court sits, if you are agreeable."

"Yes, of course."

Dr Roberts rose and followed the usher across the hall, an extra twinge of anxiety and increased tension now added to the apprehension he already felt.

He was shown into a small room leading off the hall that contained a desk and three chairs. A middle-aged man, who seemed calm but serious, stood and thanked him for coming and invited him to sit. In another chair was a young lady who smiled at him and was introduced as a trainee barrister who was sitting in on the case.

The barrister took his seat. He spoke slowly and quietly.

"I wanted to talk to you before you begin because I think that it is high time that this case is brought down to Earth, and some common sense and real fact introduced. So far there have been two days of very aggressive questioning of all our witnesses, conducted at a fast pace, and easily confusing them: making out that what they thought they saw in the stormy night might have been misinterpreted or not seen as accurately as thought. Of course, you know the charge, which does not concern any of the intended animal theft, but is solely about the arrest of the man who has brought this case to court, and the alleged assault made on him. A most improbable scenario, but from our point of view it has to be disproved. The prosecution, on the other hand, has to prove their point beyond all reasonable doubt.

First let me show you what the plaintiff and the prosecution have decided is the size of the metal rod that the police were alleged to have hammered into his ear."

He picked up a solid metal rod off the desk and handed it to him. It was straight, rounded, fifteen to twenty centimetres long, and the flattened ends were just over half a centimetre wide.

"Now perhaps you could describe to me the anatomy of the ear and what would happen if this rod were hammered into it. The jury would need this sort of detail if sensible conclusions are to be drawn."

These factors were discussed for a while in a quiet atmosphere of great seriousness. Time was short. The court would soon sit.

Eventually the barrister thanked Dr Roberts and released him back to the hall. He felt more apprehensive than ever. Appearing in court as a witness is nerve-wracking anyway: the usher coming to the door to the hall and loudly calling one's name; the walk into the crowded room all eyes turned towards the new arrival; the climb up the steps into the witness box, where the witness usually has to remain standing; the swearing with a hand on the Bible to "tell the truth, the whole truth and nothing but the truth." Then the judge asks the prosecuting counsel to address the witness.

The barrister stands up in his wig and gown, turns towards the witness, and begins.

The jury occupies two rows of bench seats, one behind the other, facing the witness box from across the other side of the court. The judge sits on a high grand wooden seat halfway along the court on the left, and below him sit the court officers, one recording everything said. On the right are the defending counsel and assistants, facing the judge, sitting on benches near the witness box. The prosecuting counsel and assistants also face the judge, seated on benches nearer to the jury. Between them and the judge is an open space.

The prosecuting counsel always begins by stating the witness's name and occupation, and the witness has to confirm that these facts are true – if they are – when counsel pauses after each question. In this case he then asked Dr Roberts if he had been requested to attend such-and-such a police station, on such-and-such a day and time, to examine etc. etc. … "and did you do so?"

"Yes."

He then asked him to describe the events in the police station, referring to a copy of his notes that had been issued to each barrister. Again and again he attempted to find fault with what Dr Roberts said and what was written in the notes. The doctor soon realised that when the barrister's remark was to be particularly scathing a very noticeable tic would appear on the left side of his face, a twitching of the muscle beneath the left eye, and the tension mounted as the next comment was awaited.

This continued for a whole hour.

Finally, because he particularly disagreed with what the doctor had just said, the barrister burst out loudly and in strong rebuke: "No! You really can not say that, it's just not right to do so!"

Suddenly the judge sat up straight and leaned forward across his desk. Until that moment he had sat back, rather slumped in his seat. According to reports he had not interfered with the prosecuting counsel and his aggressive questioning at any stage.

"Mr. (he said the barrister's name) I am the one person in this court who may decide whether what people say is not allowed. You do not have that right. The witness is giving evidence under oath and the court will consider what is said." This stern rebuke was delivered in a strong voice.

There was a pause while he looked steadfastly at the

Counsel. The latter immediately looked flustered and bowed his head.

"I apologise, My Lord, and withdraw those remarks."

A pause.

"Do you have any further questions, Mr...?" this said in a voice that rather implied that no more should be made.

"No, My Lord," said the barrister and sat down.

The judge turned to the defending counsel.

"Mr. (his name), do you wish to cross-question the witness?"

"Yes, if you please, My Lord."

The judge nodded.

Looking at Dr Roberts the counsel made a few introductory comments and asked some opening routine questions, then asked: "Dr Roberts, would you please explain to the jury the anatomy of the ear, where the injury was alleged to have been caused."

The doctor looked straight at the jury as he gave his description. He did this deliberately because in the past, when he had first attended court, the temptation had always been to look at the judge while giving evidence. The judge had stopped him immediately and requested that he address his remarks directly to the members of the jury, and not to him because it was they who had to receive all the information in order to make up their minds about the case. So the doctor talked across the courtroom to the jury as though he were explaining things to them face to face.

He described the outer ear and the tunnel through it leading to the eardrum in a way that they could understand. He turned the right side of his head slightly towards the jury, gripped the ear on that side gently between finger and thumb, and moved it about.

"As you know, the ear you can see is soft and can be moved. The opening in the ear is the start of a tunnel leading down to the eardrum, a membrane that closes off its inner end. The first part of the tunnel is soft and mobile, being part of the outer ear. By contrast the inner part is rigid, being made of bone. There is a lining over the bone that extends down to the eardrum. But the tunnel is not straight. There is an angle where the soft and hard parts meet. So a doctor looking into the tunnel with a special instrument that has a light is unable to see the eardrum unless he grips the ear at the top as I have done, and draws it gently up and towards the top of the back of the head. This manoeuvre straightens out the tunnel."

"Thank you, doctor," said the defence counsel.

"Please hand to the doctor the exhibit that is the metal rod," he requested.

An usher did so.

"It has been agreed, doctor, that this corresponds in size to the metal rod alleged to have been used. Would it have been possible to insert such a rod into the tunnel you have just described."

Again the doctor addressed the jury directly.

"There can be quite a variation in the size of the entrance to the tunnel, and of its width down to the eardrum, usually corresponding to the size of the person. Some tunnels are wide at the entrance but may narrow part way down. That of one ear may differ in size and configuration from that of the other ear in the same person. But this rod is too wide to pass much beyond the entrance to any tunnel."

"Thank you, doctor. If such a rod were placed against, or into, the entrance to the plaintiff's ear, as alleged, and hammered against it, what would be the result?"

"There would be considerable damage."

"Would you be more specific about the nature of the damage?"

"The soft part of the entrance to the tunnel, bearing in mind the angle it forms with the bony part, would be crushed against the bony area, causing bruising and most likely bleeding, and then swelling of the tissues and lining. The bone may be fractured."

"Doctor, you attended the police station on the night in question being requested to examine the plaintiff?"

"Yes I did."

"What did you examine?"

"I had been told that he had pain in the head. When

I asked him where the pain was he did not reply, but then touched his left ear. So I examined all of the head and neck, eyes, ears, nose, mouth, jaws, and all movements of these parts. He cooperated, but refused to say anything."

"Did he appear to be in pain?"

"No. He did not flinch at all during my examination."

"When you examined his ears, did you look inside them?"

"Yes, I did. I used the auroscope, which is the instrument with a light used to look into the ear."

"Did he seemed distressed when examined?"

"No."

"Did you see evidence of any injury to either ear, any bruising, swelling or bleeding?"

"No."

"I see from the records that you examined him just over two hours after the arrest. If there had been any such injury, would the evidence of it or the discomfort have disappeared in that time?"

"No."

The doctor had looked at counsel as he asked each question, and then he had turned to look steadily at the jury as he delivered his replies with a definite assurance.

"Thank you doctor." The barrister sat down.

The judge looked at both counsels.

"Are there any further questions for this witness?"

"No My Lord." This confirmed from both.

"Very well then," said the judge. He looked towards Dr Roberts. "Thank you doctor, you may stand down." The doctor turned and descended gratefully from the witness box. He had been there for just over two hours!

As he passed the defence counsel that man was studying his notes, but the trainee barrister sitting behind him was smiling broadly at Dr Roberts. Clearly she considered the session to have been a real success.

Some time later a letter arrived at Dr Roberts' surgery, sent by the firm of solicitors in London that had acted on behalf of the police. The firm was very pleased to announce that the jury had decided that the charge against the police should be dropped, and that this result was due in large part to the evidence given by Dr Roberts in court. In view of this it would be happy to honour any reasonable fee that Dr Roberts would like to suggest. The court had already paid the routine fee for the doctor's attendance, so this was an additional and unusual reward for a court appearance that had completely changed the course and outlook of the case. The firm's clients had been saved a great deal of money.

Dr Roberts had been, as all police surgeons are, summoned by the court as a neutral witness, not as one to support either the prosecution or the defence, but to provide medical evidence. This he had done. He knew that the duty of each counsel was always to act in the client's best interests to the best of his, or her, ability. In this case the prosecution had clearly lacked positive fact to work with, and so had resorted to aggressive bluster in the attempt to discredit whatever the witnesses for the defence put forward, to spike the case for the defence. But he felt pleased to have been able to assist in what, to his mind, was a just result.

Justice had been done and been seen to be done.

Also by David Forsyth

GAS MASKS, GALAXIES AND TIME